I0768734

STOLEN

By Colleen Bergquist

Copyright © 2024 by Colleen Bergquist

All rights reserved.

K & A Publishing supports the copyrights of human authors. Thank you for reading an authorized edition of this book and for complying with the copyright laws by not reproducing, scanning, or distributing any part of it in any form without written permission from the author.

This is a work of fiction. Names, characters, businesses, places, events, locales, and incidents are either the products of the author's imagination or used in a fictitious manner. Any resemblance to actual persons, living or dead, or actual events is purely coincidental.

CONTENT WARNING: The main character in this book has been a victim of child kidnapping. If this may be triggering for you, please put your mental health first and proceed with caution or skip this story completely.

eBook Edition ISBN-13: 979-8-9912505-0-5

Paperback ISBN-13: 979-8-9912504-1-2

Cover design by Elijah Toten

"When in doubt, go to the library."

Hermione Granger, Harry Potter and The Chamber of Secrets

CONTENTS

Chapter 1

I had never questioned who I was. I mean, why would I have? I was just a kid who was being raised by a single mom. It had always been the two of us. She and I were really close, and I told her everything. Until I found that newspaper clipping and discovered her secret.

I remember the day well. I was with my friend Megan, doing schoolwork in my bedroom. She attended Eastview Middle School, just down the street from the apartment complex where we both lived. I didn't go there myself as my mom homeschooled me. I met her one day while doing laundry on a Saturday afternoon, just a month after we moved to our new apartment. My mom was working. I could not leave the apartment, but after accidentally spilling something on a favorite top, I washed it with some other clothes. Megan, who was also doing laundry, struck up a conversation with me. In the time we had lived there, I had left our apartment a few times and always with my mom. I had seen no kids, so it was nice to meet someone my age. My mom let us hang out in one of the two apartments, but that was it. I couldn't leave our building. My mom was super overprotective of me even though I was almost 14. Megan and I had a lot of fun listening to music, painting our nails, and watching TV. We also did school work together. That afternoon, I was helping her with her math homework since I'm pretty smart at math. I felt like a normal kid, not the homeschooled freak I was. Anyway, we were sitting cross-legged on my twin-sized bed, working on our schoolwork, while listening to music play through a portable speaker Megan had hooked up to her iPhone. We had to sit on the bed, since my room was pretty tiny. It was big enough to hold a twin bed, a small desk, and a small bookshelf, where I kept a collection of books I'd picked up at the local thrift store. In fact, we furnished my entire room, and our entire apartment, with thrift store stuff. Since we moved so much, and often to a different state, we never took much with us so I had little. We just brought our clothes and a few belongings, since we just had a compact car. As for furniture, anything we owned was other people's discards. My mom gave away or sold any furniture before our next move. This last time, however, she'd rented a small truck since our move was local, and we had moved our furniture as well.

Unlike Megan's room, which was as small as mine but contained a white canopy bed that matched a dresser and desk, my room had a mismatched collection of furniture. The bed had an old brass head-board that had seen better days, as had my mattress, which was old. A neighbor had given it to us at our old place when she was moving out as we were moving in. My desk was white. It was wood and chipped quite a bit when I got it, so my mom and I had painted it one afternoon after we brought it home from the thrift store. The bookshelf had just two shelves and was a lighter, fake wood, and it was beat up. My mom had found that near the dumpster by our old apartment and had me help her bring it upstairs. I looked around my room. There was just one small window with some plain white blinds. I had little in the way of decorations, not like Megan's room, which was filled with all sorts of junk she'd collected over the years and posters of boy bands I had never heard of until I met her. My room just had tons of sketches I'd drawn. I was a pretty good artist even though I'd never taken an art class, and I spent many hours in my room laying on my faded floral comforter (another thrift store purchase) drawing in a sketch pad my mom had surprised me with one day when she got paid. I was happy about it since money was really tight and there weren't a lot of extras. Usually I would sketch on the back of pieces of junk mail or old envelopes.

"How come you're homeschooled, anyway?" Megan asked suddenly, looking up from the math problem she was trying to solve. "All the kids around here go to Eastview. I don't know anyone who gets homeschooled. No offense, but it's kind of weird. I mean, the schools here are fantastic. People move here just for them. I know my mom did. That was her priority when she and my dad split. She wanted to make sure I went to an excellent school. I've never known a kid who doesn't go to an actual school." She ran her fingers through her shoulder-length blonde hair as she talked, the blonde hair that currently had bright pink streaks in it. Megan wasn't the best math student, so of course, she often found other things to talk about when I was trying to help her with her work. She chewed on her pencil as she looked at me with her light green eyes. I envied her blond hair, even with its bright pink streaks. She stood out in a crowd. My looks were boring in comparison. I had dark brown hair that fell halfway down my back and brown eyes just like my mom, not that we looked very much alike. I had always assumed I look more like my dad, but there were no pictures of him anywhere in our apartment and none of my mom and I. Apparently there had been a fire in one apartment we had lived in back when we'd lived in California and we had lost a lot of our stuff. I think I had been about three or four then. I vaguely remember living in a small apartment right by the beach for a short time. But we had lived in so many places in my life and moved so often that I really could not remember details about any of them. I realized Megan was still looking at me, waiting for an answer.

"I don't know," I said. "It's what I have always done," I said. "My mom always says it's because I'm so smart and would get bored in a class full of kids. This way I get to work at my pace. We move so much anyway. Changing schools every few months would be a pain."

"Why do you move so often?" Megan asked. "I would hate that. I can't imagine living in a new place every few months and having to start over and make new friends. Doesn't your mom get how much that stinks? I was mad enough when we had to move a few years ago, but the apartment rent was going up and my mom couldn't afford it as a single parent since my deadbeat dad hardly ever pays child support. I was so happy my mom could find this place and keep me in the same school as my friends." That was one thing Megan and I had in common, no dad in our lives, but unlike mine, who I'd never met, hers drifted in and out of her life every few years. Apparently, he was in Florida now, working as a surf instructor. Her mom was young like mine and had been married for a few years. Like my mom, she worked full time, but she had a job as a secretary in a big office downtown, some place she had worked for years. My mom worked as a server at a local diner. No matter where we lived, she worked as a server.

I just laughed. "My mom doesn't care. She gets bored living in one place, says there are too many places to see, and no reason to stay in one place for too long. She loves to pick up and move with little notice. I'm lucky we've been here as long as we have. We were in Denver for five months, and we've been in Falls Creek for longer now. I'm kind of surprised we haven't moved again. I keep waiting for her to come home one day, announce she is quitting her job and then we get ready to pack our stuff and move again, not that I have much stuff," I said, looking around the room again.

"Maybe you guys can stay here and your mom will let you go to Eastview with me, instead of being homeschooled," Megan said hopefully. "We would have so much fun hanging out at school, going to basketball games, walking to the pizza place with the other kids after school..."

Knowing my mom would never go for it, I sighed, realizing that going to school wouldn't be an option. I had asked once, when I was five or six years old. We had been living in Texas then, in a small town outside of Fort Worth. One day I saw a bunch of kids outside our apartment window walking with backpacks. I had asked my mom if I could go to school, too. The next day she came home with some workbooks and announced she would be homeschooling me. When I was a lot younger, I went along to work with her since she couldn't afford babysitters.

Since she worked in small diners, the owners never seemed to care that she brought me to work with her. I'd sit at an empty booth in the corner and she'd have me work on some workbooks, stopping over to help me when the diner got slow. Sometimes if she worked an early morning shift, she'd have me nap on my coat in the back room away from the noise. She always seemed to have an understanding boss. Then again, my mom seemed to talk people into stuff pretty easily. We hadn't even had to put much of a security deposit on the current apartment. She had given the landlord some sob story about how she was a single mom running from her abusive ex-husband. She told him she had a job lined up and a little money, but we had left in the middle of the night with just a few belongings. The landlord believed her. We had just two small bags between us when we arrived late one afternoon. Later that night, once it was dark, we'd walked down the street to where she had parked the car to move it to the entrance so we could unload the trailer we had rented. Of course, the landlord wasn't there to see that we were not as badly off as she had claimed to get the apartment.

We had internet access, so I could go online and learn stuff too. We'd always get a library card too, and I read lots of books. Mostly I just worked on reading and math since she could get workbooks, but now that I was older it was getting harder as she didn't have the skills to teach me since she only had a high school education. Apparently, she'd gotten pregnant with me right out of high school and her foster parents had kicked her out of the house. She never talked much about my dad, so I figured he was some guy she had dated in high school, or maybe just after. Anyway, we didn't need him. My mom and I had always gotten along just fine without him.

"Emma, I'm being serious. You need to talk with your mom about this." Megan's voice cut into my thoughts again. "You're 13 now, almost 14. High school is just around the corner and it would be so great to have you at school with me. We would have a great time. Besides, you said yourself that you mostly teach yourself things by watching videos and going online. That's not the same as going to school and being taught by teachers."

Megan made a good argument, but I knew it would never happen. "You know my mom would never go for it," I said. "I'm lucky she lets us hang out. She wasn't thrilled when she found out I left the apartment the day I met you. She would never let me leave the apartment to go to school. I can't even go down to the corner coffee shop unless she is with me. She has been looking into enrolling me in virtual high school, but it's kind of expensive, so I doubt we can afford it."

"Virtual high school?" Megan asked, wrinkling her nose. "What is that? Like high school online? That doesn't sound very fun. What do you do? Just sit at a computer all day and do your work? That's no different from what you do now. How do you meet any kids?"

"I think there are some live classes, so I could talk with kids and the teacher during those," I said. "My mom just started looking into it. With me getting older, she doesn't know enough to teach me, so I'm basically teaching myself. It's a good thing I'm naturally good at Math, because I go online to Khan Academy and teach myself algebra."

Megan looked at me like I was crazy. "Well, I'm glad you are good at math so you can help me. I had better finish my homework. My mom will kill me if she sees it not done after I told her you and I were going to do it together." I had to laugh because Megan got distracted really easily. I looked at the time on my phone. It was almost time for me to make dinner.

After Megan and I finished our assignments, she walked to her apartment down the hall and kept thinking about what she and I had talked about. Why couldn't I go to Eastview? It actually made sense. It was right down the street and it probably cost less than the virtual school she was looking into. I just had to figure out how to convince her.

Chapter 2

While I waited for my mom, I relaxed on my bed and admired the simple decor of my small bedroom. Moving frequently teaches you that you can't have many things. Perhaps my mom would consider staying in Falls Creek for a while, now that we'd been here a few months and I was getting older. I got tired of moving and not having people my age around. I didn't feel like leaving now that I had made a friend. I closed my eyes and thought about how I could bring up the possibility of me going to school.

Right at 5:00, she came home and we settled down at our tiny kitchen table to eat. Sitting down to have dinner with her was something I really enjoyed, and we did it most nights. With her long hours at the diner and occasional night shifts for extra money, it was our only opportunity to sit down and chat.

Most of the time, I could talk with her about anything, but this was hard. I knew she was against me going to school. She never allowed me to go anywhere without her. Once or twice, Megan had invited me to go out with her friends, and she always said no. She was overly cautious, thinking it was unsafe for me to step foot outside the apartment, which was absurd since I was not a young child. I wanted to bring up the idea of school, but just didn't know how to get the conversation started. I decided to talk about some other things. Maybe I could start by telling her how much I loved living here. Yeah, that might work. I'd start out talking about that and then spring the school thing on her.

I started by asking my mom about her day, knowing she loved sharing little stories about the customers, many of whom were regulars who came into the diner every day. I loved listening to her stories. It made me feel connected with the outside world, something I didn't always feel since I spent most of my time cooped up in our two bedroom apartment. I spent my days doing schoolwork, reading, and watching TV. I would have loved to go out and explore, but of course that was forbidden. Sometimes on the weekends, we would take the Light Rail into the city to check out a local festival or just walk around, but money was pretty tight so we only did stuff if it was free or cheap. I only went places if she was with me.

That evening as I helped myself to some ravioli and salad I had thrown together before she got home from work, I brought up the topic of school with my mom, but I knew I needed to choose my words carefully. Just as I'd planned, I started by telling her how much I loved living where we did.

"I'm so glad we moved to Falls Creek. It's such a great town and I'm so glad we moved out of the city. It's so nice here. This apartment is great and I love finally having a friend right down the hall. In the city, there were no kids my age in our building." It was funny, I thought, my mom always seemed to rent apartments in buildings with no kids. I hadn't thought about that until recently. When she said nothing, I added, "Seriously Mom, I love Falls Creek and I hope we can stay here for awhile, maybe even until I finish high school."

My mom gave me a strange look. "What on earth brought this on? Sure, Falls Creek is nice, but there are a lot of great towns in Colorado. Maybe we'll move closer to the mountains, get an apartment there, but that's pretty expensive. Maybe I can get a job at a ski resort restaurant. I hear sometimes those jobs include housing. Who knows if we will stay in Colorado? Maybe we'll leave this snow and cold behind and head back to California. I miss the beach. It would be fun to go there on my days off."

I looked at her in horror. This conversation was quickly taking a bad turn. I started talking about how much I loved living in Falls Creek and my mom started saying we should move again. "No Mom, we can't move! I love it here. Besides, Megan is here and she's my only friend. I'm tired of moving. We move all the time. I can't even remember how many places we have lived."

My mom sighed. "I'm glad you and Megan have become such good friends over the past few months. It's nice you have a friend your own age to hang out with for a bit, but you can't get too attached. You know we never live in one place too long. I signed a month to month lease on purpose. We can move any time."

I sighed. This conversation was definitely heading the wrong way. If I didn't get her mind off moving and fast, she would have us packed up and moving out, and I'd never see Megan again. "Mom, I feel like this would be a great year for me to attend school like other kids do, especially since you really can't help me with school work much anymore." I waited in silence, biting on my lower lip, wondering what she would say. For a minute, she just looked at me. Then she picked up her fork, ate a bite of her ravioli, put down the fork and looked at me.

"Absolutely not, Emma," she said sharply. "There is no reason for you to go to public school. You've always learned at home and it's what is best for you. I know you're at the age when it's getting hard for me to teach you, but there are other ways for you to learn. I've been looking into one of those virtual high schools we talked about. Did you know you can work at your own pace and sometimes graduate even faster? Plus if you do well, you can take more advanced classes."

"Why would I want to do that? If I go to school at Eastview I get to be with other kids and with teachers who know the different subjects. Why is homeschooling best for me Mom? I'm always by myself, never around any other kids except for Megan. You won't even let me go with her when she hangs out with her friends. I think it would be kind of fun to go to school. I'd get to be in classes with a bunch of other kids, make some other friends, and join some after school clubs." I waited, feeling confident that I'd made some good arguments. Surely my mom had to think about it.

"What brought this on?" my mom asked quietly. "You never brought up any of this before. I thought you enjoyed being home-schooled."

"Well Megan and I were talking..." my voice trailed off and I switched gears and focused on why being in school would be better for me. I didn't want her to think this was all Megan's idea.

"Forget about going to school with friends and think about this. I'm 13, almost 14. College is a few years away," I said, knowing us affording college was unlikely. Unless I could get some scholarships, I would end up working some dead end, boring job like my mom. "It would probably help me get in if I went to an excellent school. There's a few months left in the school year, Maybe I could go to Eastview and see how it goes. You know, like a trial run before high school this Fall?"

My mom was silent for several minutes. I smiled to myself, knowing I had made some good points. . It had been a convincing argument and one that had just come to me at the spur of the moment. Maybe, just maybe it would work. But just as quickly as I got my hopes up, my mom dashed them.

"It is different, Emma. We're talking about a whole environment change, which I'm not convinced is a good thing. Schools today are not a safe place. Look at all of the shootings that have been on the news and a few of those have been here in Colorado. I would worry about you too much. It's why I don't let you leave our apartment without me. At least with you doing school work at home, I know where you are and that you are safe. If you were in a big public school and something happened I would never forgive myself. You are all I have and I cannot lose you."

"Seriously Mom? That is the craziest thing I have ever heard. Sure, there are shootings in schools, but there are shootings in diners too and you work in one. How is that any different from me attending a school? Maybe we should avoid going to any public place if they're not safe. I mean there are movie theaters, museums, restaurants..."

My mom interrupted me. "Emma, I will not get into a debate with you. I am an adult. You are the child and I will decide what's best for you and what I think is best is for you to continue being homeschooled."

"I am not a child," I screamed. "You just insist on treating me like one." I could not stand to be in the room with her another second. Standing up, I pushed in my chair and stomped off to my bedroom and closed the door, ignoring her pleas to sit down and talk about this calmly.

I was lying on my bed, music cranked up and earbuds in my ears, when my mom walked in and pulled out the earbuds, standing next to my bed. I glared up at her.

"Your behavior was completely uncalled for. I'm sorry that you are mad, but as a parent, I won't always make decisions you'll agree with, but I am doing what is best for you," she said. "I decided a long time ago that homeschooling meets our needs and I'm not changing that decision just because you've decided you want to go to school to meet more kids and hang out with them. I already let you hang out with Megan. That should be enough for you."

"How is sitting in an apartment all day by myself doing schoolwork and never interacting with other kids best for me?" I asked. "I have almost no interaction with other kids. Megan is my only friend and if she didn't live down the hall, I would have no one to hang out with and would be completely alone all the time, just like I was in Denver and the other places we've lived."

"You are not always by yourself Emma. If I don't have a shift, I am here with you a lot of times, and you and Megan find plenty of time to hang out when she's not at school." Ugh, I was so frustrated! There had to be a way to convince her that going to school with Megan was a good idea.

"Yeah, again I just have Megan and we hang out when she isn't in school or out with her other friends. You never even let me go anywhere without you. Last weekend when Megan was going to the movies with some friends from school, you wouldn't let me join them. You could at least let me meet other kids. I would like more than one friend."

"I told you I am not comfortable with 13 year olds going off to the movies by themselves. You're just too young. It's not safe for a bunch of young teens to run around unsupervised like that." I rolled my eyes at that comment. I saw plenty of young teens hanging out without parents. It seemed like I was the only one with her mother within a few feet of her when we left the apartment. She treated me like such a baby.

Still, I understood that mentioning all the other children were permitted would be pointless. An entire childhood of living with a super controlling, overprotective mother had taught me that. No matter where we lived, I could never do much of anything.When I was younger, my mom had never let me play at neighborhood parks, and we didn't go to huge, public places like malls or amusement parks. We mostly kept to ourselves, and because we moved so often and lived in places with no kids, I didn't meet any. My mom even kept to herself at work. She never bothered getting to know any of the people she worked with or even our neighbors. She always said there was no point since we wouldn't live there long.

"Okay, so you like homeschooling. Have you ever considered maybe I don't like it anymore? I'm getting older now. I need more of a challenge. School can give me that. There are so many classes I can take in school: art, music, drama, cooking, and computers. Megan told me kids in middle school and high school get to choose whatever classes they want. Her older cousin told her. It sounds amazing!"

My mom was looking irritated with me, something I'd rarely seen before. I had upset her. I felt a bit guilty, until I heard what she had to say next.

"Emma, homeschooling works for us because we can do it anywhere. I love that I don't have to pull you out of school if we decide to up and move to a new place. We don't have a lot of stuff so we can move quickly, and it's always been easy to find a job since there are tons of little diners and restaurants all over. I can find a new job when we decide to move."

"When WE decide to move? When have I ever had a choice? It's always you coming home one day and deciding we're moving again. When we left the city after five months, I woke up one morning expecting you were leaving for work and you were packing our stuff.

You told me we were moving to the suburbs. You never ask me if I WANT to move. We just do. Why do we move all the time anyways? Would it be so bad to stay in one place forever? Why do we have to keep moving to new places? I hate moving so much!"

"Oh Emma," my mom laughed. "You know I'd never be happy staying in one place for too long. There are just too many places to see. Life is all about having adventures and seeing new places. Think about all of the great places where we have lived. You have gotten to live by the beach, live in the desert, and see mountains. How many kids your age could say the same thing?"

"Can you just leave me alone?" I asked, growing more and more annoyed with her by the minute. "Obviously you don't want to take my feelings into consideration. I should know by now I never get an opinion about anything!" I picked up my earbuds and glared at her, wishing she would just leave me alone. I just knew any day now she was going to have us move again. For all I knew, she might have already started planning our next move.

My mom looked like she wanted to say something, but she just nodded and walked away, leaving me to my music. I stuck the earbuds back in my ear. I was just so ticked off at her right now. I ran my hands through my long brown hair and tapped my right hand along to the beat of the rock music that blasted through my earbuds. I just did not get my mom sometimes. It wasn't like what I was asking for was such a big deal. Lots of kids my age went to school. Why couldn't I? What was the big deal? I knew she was overprotective of me, but this forbidding me from going to school ever was a bit much even for her. It made me wonder if there was more going on than I realized. Surely this couldn't be just about school, could it?

CHAPTER 3

The next morning I woke early, not that I had slept well. It had taken me a long time to fall asleep after the argument with my mom. That she refused to be reasonable and discuss the idea bothered me. Her behavior was very out of character. Since it had always been just the two of us, we'd always talked things over and she had always given me a chance to express my opinion about things. Until now, and it bothered me.

I was still thinking about things as I sat down at breakfast a little while later. "You're kind of quiet this morning," my mom said, placing her coffee mug on the table and sitting across from me. I just shrugged and slowly dragged my spoon through the milk I had poured into my cereal. I really did not want to get into another argument like we had the night before.

"Seriously Emma. You're not still mad about last night, are you?" she asked.

"Not mad, just confused. It's like you won't even discuss the idea of me going to school. You just shut down the idea without talking about it. It's like you won't even listen to me. I gave you a lot of good reasons. Going to school would be a good idea. You could at least say you will consider it."

"It's not something I feel we need to discuss. If you feel you need interaction with other kids, we'll enroll you in the virtual school online for this fall and you can chat with the other students. It would be just like going to school."

I rolled my eyes. As if that was the same as me going to an actual school with actual students and having actual conversations, belonging to school clubs, and going to school sporting events.

"Mom, it's not just about going to school and you know it. I want to be AROUND other kids, not just chatting with them online. I want to hang out with them at lunch, be in after-school clubs with them, and maybe go to some games. Why are you being so weird about this? It's just school."

"To you, it's just school, Emma. To me, it's sending you out to a place where you might not be safe. The world is a dangerous place. Look at the news. There are many kidnappings and shootings. Nothing can happen to you because you are in our apartment or down in Megan's apartment. At school, you are away from me all day and anything could happen to you. I need to keep you safe Emma and you learning at home helps me do that. If you leave the apartment without me, I cannot keep you safe."

I stood up angrily. "You cannot just keep me in a bubble my entire life, Mom!" I yelled. "I'm 13, not three. I need to be around other kids, and I need to go to school and not just some virtual online school, but an actual school in an actual building. It's time to cut the apron strings a bit and stop treating me like a baby!"

My mom sighed. I knew it was wrong to lose my temper with her for the second time in two days, but I did not get her reasoning at all.

Sure, she'd always been quite overprotective of me for as long as I could remember. It was getting ridiculous. It's not like I was asking to go wander all over the city. I just wanted to go to a school a few blocks away like other kids my age. I wanted to be a normal teenager.

My mom glanced at me, and we sat in silence while eating. I finished, excused myself, went into the bedroom, and shut the door. I just could not be around her anymore. She was annoying me way too much and in the past two days, she and I had argued more than we had my entire life.

Later that morning, my mom was cleaning our apartment, and I was sitting down working through a new language arts workbook my mom had picked up for me. I didn't feel like doing any work. I suppose that was one positive thing about being homeschooled. There were no teachers dictating my assignments. Even my mom left me alone most of the time. When we had moved to Denver last year, she had picked up some textbooks for my grade level at a library sale. She wasn't a teacher, so mostly she had me reading things in the books and writing about what I learned. Sometimes we talked about things I was reading or the math I was doing, but rarely. I did my work on my own, which had always been fine with me. Of course, I had known nothing different. It had just never bothered me until now.

Maybe it was that I was about to turn 14, and hearing Megan talk about middle school, which she would finish up this year. She had been telling me stories about keeping your books in a locker and having different teachers for different subjects. Plus, middle school meant going to football and basketball games, joining after-school clubs, and hanging out with your friends after school. High school had even more things kids could do. Megan was so excited, and while I was excited for her, I wanted to have all that, too. I just had to convince my mom. Sighing, I turned back to the book, but I wasn't in the mood to work. I put on my earbuds and listened to music, but it wasn't long before my mom interrupted me.

"Emma, my boss called. Lisa's sick. I need to go in earlier today. Are you okay on your own, or do you want to come and hang out at the diner for a few hours?"

"No thanks, I'm fine here Mom," I said, resisting the urge to roll my eyes. I hadn't hung out while she worked for over a year now. We had agreed I was old enough to hang out on my own. It wasn't like I could go anywhere ever, unless you counted going down the hall to Megan's apartment, which I didn't.

Once she'd left for work, I went online and looked up the high school website to see if I could find out more about going there next year. I clicked on a link that said "9th Grade" and saw information about all the classes kids took. Of course, there were the usual things like Language Arts, Math, Social Studies, and Science, but there also was information about the "Electives" Megan's cousin had told her about. There were so many! Every student got to choose two elective classes each year. There were classes in Spanish, French, Technology, Music, Art (So many art classes!), digital design, and robotics. Those were not things I got to do as a homeschooled kid. Then there were all the different clubs and activities after school, not to mention sports teams I could join. I needed to convince my mom that it was time to make a change. Maybe once I showed her all the different classes I could take, and she saw how excited I was, she would agree. I mean, it wasn't like she could teach me all those things. She was always saying I should learn new things, and this was my chance.

Since she had been so against the idea, I did some more research before I approached her again. I clicked on the link that said "Registration" and learned all I needed was proof of address (my mom's driver's license and a copy of our lease) as well as my birth certificate.

Then there was a short emergency form my mom needed to fill out and a small fee to cover the cost of textbooks. Since my mom earned little money, they could even waive that. It all seemed very easy, except for the part where I had to convince her to let me go.

I opened the registration form and printed a copy. Carrying it, I went to the living room and set it on my mom's desk. I sat down and opened the file drawer where she kept important papers, such as paid bills and our apartment lease. I knew my birth certificate was probably there, although I'd never seen it. I hesitated for a minute. I'd never gone into that drawer, much less taken anything out of it, and I wasn't sure I should do it now. But then again, it's not like I was snooping. I was just getting something my mom would need to get anyway if she agreed to enroll me in school. The way I saw it, filling out the paperwork and getting the birth certificate out was just saving her time.

Careful not to disturb anything, I began looking through the files to find what I needed. There was not much there, just a file with copies of our paid bills over the past year and a copy of our lease. A file behind that said personal. That had to be what I needed. I opened the thin folder that contained just a few things. The first was a birth certificate, but it belonged to my mom. There was another paper stuck behind it and I grabbed it, thinking it was my birth certificate, but it wasn't. It was a newspaper article. That was weird. Why would my mom have put a newspaper article in a file marked Personal? Curious, I removed the article and read it.

Toddler Abducted From Chicago Park

Chicago Police are investigating the disappearance of a three-year-old girl from Bessie Coleman Park yesterday afternoon. The girl, Emily Ann Miller of Chicago, was at the park with her mother and two sisters when she disappeared. The girl's mother, Nancy Miller, said the girls were playing for about 30 minutes while she sat on a nearby bench talking with a friend. Her two young daughters came up crying and told her a woman had grabbed Emily and ran off with her. Police were called, and an extensive search of the park and surrounding area turned up no sign of either Emily or the unknown woman. People are being asked to be on the lookout and contact police if they see anyone who looks like Emily or the woman.

I studied the grainy photograph accompanying the article. It was of a girl with dark brown hair parted to one side and clipped back with a barrette. I stared at the article again. Why on earth did my mom have it, and why was it hidden away in the back of a file cabinet behind her birth certificate? I looked at the article again, seeing if there was anything there that might help me. It seemed that someone had torn it out of a newspaper, and they had also cut off the date. However, the slightly yellowed paper led me to believe that it was an older article. But how old? And what paper did it come out of? I assumed someone must have taken it from a Chicago newspaper, but we'd never lived in Chicago, at least not that I could remember. We had always lived in the Southwest part of the country, as my mom preferred warmer weather. So how would she have gotten a Chicago newspaper and why would she have torn out and saved this article?

I looked at it one more time, puzzled. Was this someone she knew? Maybe a friend's child or a relative? I was confused. I knew my mom had been a foster kid so it couldn't be a relative and I didn't remember my mom ever making friends anywhere we had lived. I stared at the grainy photograph on the yellowed newspaper, wondering who Emily Ann Miller was, and why my mom had a newspaper article about her in a hidden file folder labeled personal?

Chapter 4

I lost track of time as I stood there, gripping the article and lost in thought. I was completely clueless about what to do. Should I show the article to my mom and ask her about it? I couldn't do it, as I would have to justify why I was searching through her desk drawer and files. I had no reason to use my mom's desk or computer since I had my own. There would be no reason for me to sit at my mom's desk, and definitely no reason to snoop through files and remove something. I made a copy and then decided to put the newspaper article back. After doing so, I returned the original back to its hiding place, made sure nothing else looked out of place, and took the copy to my room where I could study it more.

Even after rereading the article, I was still confused. I needed to uncover more information about the missing girl and understand why my mother had an old newspaper article about her kidnapping. I had an idea. I might find additional information through online research. Maybe I'll do a search using this girl's name to see if I find anything. I picked up my laptop from the desk, logged in, and opened my browser. I typed in "Emily Ann Miller" and "Chicago kidnapping" and received several hits right away.

A majority of them seemed to be reports focused on her disappearance and the ongoing investigation. Next, there was something that caught my attention. It appeared to be an updated story, published just a few days before.

Family Marks 10th Anniversary of Girl's Disappearance

Three-year-old Emily Ann Miller hasn't been seen in a decade. Taken from a busy playground, the dark-haired toddler disappeared suddenly, leaving her parents and the Chicago community to wonder what became of her. Following the suspected abduction, police concentrated on sightings of a girl who looked like Emily with a dark haired woman on a path. The entire park and its surroundings were thoroughly searched, but no sign of Emily or her suspected abductor was found. Over the following weeks, an extensive search was carried out in the Chicago area, and later expanded nationwide.

Even though the little girl disappeared years ago, Emily's parents still hold onto hope for her return.

Nancy Miller stated firmly that they would never give up. "Both Sean and I genuinely believe that our daughter is out there waiting for us. All we want is for her to be with us at home with us at home. We strongly believe she is alive, possibly residing with the woman we suspect took her."

The Chicago Police released an age progression sketch to show what Emily might look like now, considering she was abducted 10 years ago as a young girl.

Shocked, my mouth fell open as I looked at the sketch. The resemblance was so uncanny, it was like staring at myself. It was as if the missing girl and I were identical twins. Her hair and facial features were so similar to mine that it felt like I was looking at a twin. The description mentioned dark brown hair, brown eyes, and a small jagged scar above her right eyebrow.

How was that even possible? It's said that everyone has a look-alike, but it was mind-blowing when a girl who had been missing for years had an age progression picture that looked exactly like me. What's more, the missing girl was also 13 years old, just like me. However, she was from Chicago while I came from California. That girl couldn't possibly be me.

I continued to sit silently, pondering further. Was it possible that I was this girl? Is that why my mom had the article hidden away? Had she lied to me about having me right after high school? What if I had been abducted at three and taken far from Chicago, and the woman I thought was my mom was actually a kidnapper? No. It seemed like a bizarre coincidence that I bore a resemblance to the girl who went missing in Chicago. It was difficult to believe. I already knew my identity. There had to be a logical explanation for this.

I closed the web browser after printing out the story. I pulled the picture out of the printer and stared at the age progression drawing once more. My hair was longer and I had a different hairstyle. Yet, the face was unmistakable. Mine was a perfect match for the one in the sketch. As I studied the picture more closely, I discovered something I overlooked at first. Just like me, the girl in the photo had a small scar above her eyebrow. There's no way that could have been a coincidence. How many girls of the same age could possibly have matching hair color, eye color, and an identical scar in the same spot?

I couldn't remember a time when I didn't have that scar. My mom said that I fell and got a cut on the edge of a coffee table when I was learning to walk. The scar was from a few stitches I'd gotten.

I felt puzzled as I stared at my own reflection. I reached out and studied the scar. I glanced at the newspaper photo and Emily's scar. Identical. There's no way that's just a coincidence. It's possible to resemble someone else, even be their identical twin, but having the exact same scar in the exact same spot seems unlikely. It wasn't possible. I was starting to freak out.

I stashed the two articles inside a book and carefully returned the book to my bookshelf. I started pacing in my small bedroom, thinking. I had to talk with someone. Megan, I thought. I could trust her, and it's not like I could ask my mom.

Sadly, Megan wouldn't be home from school for another hour. That hour felt like it would never end. I filled my time by reading the two articles and searching the internet for any additional articles regarding the disappearance of this girl. I knew Megan came home about 3:15 so I was waiting in the building's lobby by 3:10, wanting to talk with her the second I could.

"Hey! What's up?" Megan asked, walking through the lobby doors, backpack slung over her left shoulder. She looked confused. I had never waited in the lobby for her before.

"I need to talk. Now!" I grabbed her by the arm and practically pulled her towards the elevator.

"Okay, okay. Chill Emma. We'll be upstairs in a few minutes and then we can hang out in my room and talk," Megan said.

"No! Not your room," I said, the panicked feeling coming back. "My apartment. My mom's at work so we'll have privacy there for what I need to show you."

"Privacy? You need to show me something? Emma, this is getting weirder by the minute. What's up?" She asked as the elevator doors opened and we got on, both pressing the button for the 5th floor at the same time.

"Not here," I said. "Just tell your mom we need to do something, like you need my help with a math assignment and hurry."

On the 5th floor, the elevator stopped. Megan went in one direction while I went in the opposite. I entered the apartment and anxiously walked around the living room until Megan arrived. I flung it open quickly, let her in, and then shut the door.

"Finally! What took you so long?" I asked.

Megan laughed. "It's been like ten minutes Emma. You know how my mom is. She wanted to hear all about my day. I told her I really needed to come down and ask you for help with my math homework. She knows I'm hopeless at math, so she let me come after I promised we would study and not socialize. Anyway, you said you had to show me something."

"Yes, something big. Come in my room, but keep the door open so we'll hear my mom if she comes home early. She's not due home until 6:00, but you never know if the diner might be slow and she might come home early and I don't want her to hear our conversation."

"This is getting stranger by the minute," Megan said, heading towards my room. I followed closely, considering how to tell my lone friend about what I uncovered last night and my suspicions.

Megan wasted no time and sat on my bed as soon as we entered my room. I went to the bookshelf, grabbed the book I had placed there earlier, and joined her. Despite being alone in the apartment with an open bedroom door, I spoke in a whisper.

"So earlier today, I decided to print the registration form for Eastview and fill it out. It said I needed my birth certificate so..."

"Your mom said you can go??? That's fantastic!" Megan squealed, cutting me off.

"Would you let me finish please?" I paused for a minute, trying to find the right words. "I went into my mom's file drawer in the computer desk since I know she keeps a lot of important papers there. I found the lease for our apartment, some paid bills, her birth certificate, and...this," I said, showing her the first article, the one about Emily's abduction. I was filled with anticipation as she examined it.

"I don't get it Emma. Why would your mom have this? It says this girl was kidnapped in Chicago. Who is she? Is she someone in your family or maybe the kid of someone she knows?"

"That's what I thought, but as far as I know she's never lived in Chicago and we don't know anyone who lives there. I decided to go online and do a bit of research to see if I could find more out about this missing girl, maybe figure out why my mom might have saved the article. I don't know, maybe my mom knew the family or something."

"That's definitely strange," Megan admitted. "What about your grandparents, aunts, and uncles? Do they know anyone in Chicago? Maybe the kid belongs to a friend of theirs and they sent the article to your mom?"

I then told Megan something I'd never told anyone before. "My mom has no family. She was a foster kid until she was 17 and never knew her parents. I have no relatives, at least not that we know of. Anyway, that's not important. It's what I found on the Internet," I said, handing her the second article.

Megan read it silently and then looked at the sketch at the bottom and then at me. Her mouth opened wide as she stared at me. For once, she seemed at a loss for words. I knew she saw the resemblance between me and Emily. She had to. It was that obvious.

She fixed her gaze on me, then on the article, and then back on me. Finally, I broke the silence. "I look EXACTLY like her. Do you see it?" I asked, my voice starting to shake.

Megan's eyes remained fixed on me, then flicked back to the picture, and then back to me again. She asked, "I mean, how is that even possible? This happened 10 years ago so they have no idea what this girl Emily really looks like. I agree, the drawing bears a strong resemblance to you. It's clear that they used a childhood photo of her to age her face. No offense Emma, but you have light skin, brown eyes, and brown hair. There are many people you could resemble."

"That's what I thought too, at first, but then I saw this," I said, putting my fingernail on the scar above the girl's left eyebrow. I pushed my bangs to the side and showed Megan the very faint, but still visible scar on my face in the exact same place. She gasped. It was hidden by my hair, so she had never seen it until now.

"We both have a scar in the exact same spot. According to my mom, I got mine when I accidentally hit my face on a dresser as a child." We sat in silence for a few minutes. At long last, Megan spoke again in a barely audible whisper.

"But...if this is you, and I'm not saying it is. How is it possible that you were kidnapped a decade ago and nobody ever located you? It's not like you've been completely cut off from the world."

"But haven't I really?" I asked, thinking about all the places we had lived in my short life, how sometimes we would stay someplace for just a few months, how my mom always worked in little diners, never big chain restaurants, how I'd never been allowed to go to school, or any big public places. Did all the moves happen so no one would find me? Was I someone else?

"We move ALL THE TIME, every few months. The longest I have lived anywhere was a year and a half when we lived in that tiny town in Wyoming before we moved to Denver last year. Then we were there a few months when my mom decided on a whim to move to Falls Creek."

Megan nodded, but then said, "You said your mom hates living in the same place. She's a waitress so she can always get a new job in a new place."

"She always works in small diners instead of big restaurants, and despite needing the money, she never considers going back to school for a better job. Take a moment to ponder this. I don't go to school. It's weird. What if there's a reason for that? I found her birth certificate, but not mine. Maybe it does not exist. What if I'm not Emma Nicole McKay, but Emily Ann Miller?"

Megan stared at me in disbelief. "But you can't be. It's crazy to think your mom isn't your mom, but some stranger that kidnapped you in Chicago and has been keeping you for 10 years, pretending to be your mom. That kind of stuff only happens in the movies."

"Clearly not," I replied, gesturing towards the article resting on the bed. "This is a real girl who was kidnapped 10 years ago, and no one has seen her since," I said, while pointing to the article that now lay on the bed between us. "Her family still thinks about her and wants to find her. They believe she is alive, and maybe she is. What if I'm not Emma, but Emily? Let's look at the facts, Megan. I live only with my mom. There's no dad in the picture or no relatives. My mom was in foster care and has no siblings. We don't stay in one place long, and every few months she comes home and announces we're moving again. Apartments that we rent are typically in buildings with either single people or old people. There's never kids my age. My mom refuses to let me attend school, and I have no friends except for you. You're the first friend I have ever met, and that happened because I left the apartment. I bet my mom looked at this apartment building and figured no kids lived here. There's no pool and no playground. It's this older building. There's nothing about it that screams it's a family place. Nothing. Don't you think that's all suspicious when I go looking for my birth certificate-something my mom should have, and all I find is a newspaper article about a missing girl who I look exactly like right down to a scar above my eyebrow?"

"You said your mom was a foster child, so that explains the no family thing," Megan said. "Yes, you move a lot and sometimes you don't move that far. Come on, you guys moved a half hour from Denver to Falls Creek. It's not like you moved across the country or something."

"True, but we've never left the Southwest. We move back and forth, always between a few states, and each of those states has one thing in common. They are far from Chicago. What if my mom isn't my mom, but some lady who kidnapped me in Chicago and moved me away across the country so no one could find me?"

"But this story went national," Megan said again. "It mentioned that they issued an Amber Alert for Emily, meaning every police department in the country was on the lookout for her and the woman who took her."

Megan had a point. If I had been kidnapped and there was a nationwide search, someone might have spotted me and alerted the police. Wouldn't they have? Or was it possible people had never seen me? Could she have kept me hidden away from people until enough time had passed? I tried to remember where we'd lived when I was three, and I couldn't. I couldn't remember much about my life then. I knew we had lived in California, Texas, New Mexico, Wyoming, and Arizona because my mom had told me, but I couldn't remember much about any of the states or my life there, except for Wyoming, where we had lived for a while before moving to Colorado.

"Earth to Emma," a voice said. I turned to look at Megan. "You're spacing out."

"I just realized I don't know where I was living at three. I can name all the different states we've lived in because my mom told me, but there have been so many towns. I can't remember anything specific except that we lived in Wyoming for a little over a year before moving to Colorado last year. How is that possible? I know we move a lot, but I should be able to remember something and I can't."

"What about pictures? Does your mom keep any photo albums around here that we could look at for clues?"

"We don't have any. My mom doesn't even own a camera, so it's not like she could take any...," my voice trailed off. It was kind of weird we didn't have any pictures, at least none that I'd ever seen. We both had phones, but she didn't take many of me, just places with scenery.

"Seriously? But what about birthdays, vacations, that kind of thing? Surely your mom must have pictures of you growing up."

"I asked my mom once, and she said we had an apartment fire when I was really little and we lost a lot of stuff." I said. "What if there are no photos of me around for a reason? If I really am someone else, she wouldn't want something like photos lying around for anyone to see. Same thing about a birth certificate. What kind of person doesn't have a birth certificate for their own kid?"

Megan and I sat there in silence for a while. Suddenly, we heard a key in the door, then a voice.

CHAPTER 5

"Emma, are you here?" I froze. It was my mom. I quickly picked up the articles, shoved them into the book, and put the book on my bookshelf. "I'm in my room with Megan. We're doing homework." I looked at Megan, who quickly opened her math book and notebook and we tried to look busy when my mom walked in a few minutes later.

"Oh Megan, how nice to see you! So what are you girls up to?"

"Actually, Emma had just finished showing me something in math. I'm so lucky to have such a good friend who can help me. I'd better go though. My mom's probably got dinner waiting. I'll see you later, Emma," Megan said, quickly gathering up her things. She caught my eye as she walked out the door and mouthed, "Talk later."

My mom sat down on the bed next to me. "I'm glad you and Megan are getting to be such good friends," she said. "It's nice for you to have someone to hang out with."

"Yes, it is. What would be nicer is to have some more friends, like the kind I would meet going to school, like the other kids around here."

My mom sighed. "Not this again, Emma. I thought we discussed this and agreed we would continue homeschooling. It's what we've always done, and it is working. Why change it now?"

"WE never agreed on anything, Mom. It's not like you ever gave me a choice in the matter. You told me when I was five it was time for me to learn some things, so you went and bought me some workbooks and you started teaching me at home. Where were we living then? Texas right? Where did we live before then?"

"Yes, Fort Worth, Texas. Why all the questions about where we lived? I can't keep track since we move a lot."

"I was just curious, that's all. I started thinking about all the places we've lived and I couldn't remember when we lived someplace or even towns we lived in. We seem to move so much. It's just not normal."

"I know there's been a lot of moves, Emma, and I blame myself for that. When I was growing up, I only lived in California and always wished I could live in a different place. I love to see fresh places so I've moved us around a lot. It's easier since it's just the two of us."

"Do you ever get the urge to move someplace in a different part of the country, like Minnesota or Chicago? Maybe someplace really different?" I asked, putting a slight emphasis on Chicago and watching her face closely, hoping somehow her reaction might give me a clue. Maybe let me know I had reason to be suspicious, but she just laughed at my suggestion.

"Those places are a bit too cold for me. I'm much happier in the Southwest. We still get the snow out this way, but the weather is a lot more mild, and it's sunny here a lot. I have no desire to move to the Midwest. Too flat and too much snow. I'm going to make dinner for us now."

The conversation was over and I had gotten no clues that would help me solve this mystery. Maybe it was crazy, but I guess I'd been hoping for some look of shock or surprise on her face when I'd mentioned Chicago, but there was none. So basically I had learned nothing more. I had a few articles on a missing girl that looked just like me and a mom who had clammed up when I tried to find out more about the places we'd lived. So basically I had nothing except a weird feeling that I couldn't shake.

***

During dinner that night, I was quiet. After Megan's reaction that afternoon, I was definitely getting suspicious. There were so many unanswered questions I had and the one person who could answer them was sitting right across from me. Yet, I couldn't ask her. How could I? What was I supposed to do, show her the newspaper article I had taken from a file in her desk and admit I had been looking through her files? No, I couldn't do that. But there had to be some way to find out if I really was Emma McKay or Emily Miller. I realized I needed a copy of my birth certificate and my mom didn't have it, so I needed to figure out how to get one. Then at least I would have proof that I was not someone else.

After dinner, my mom and I cleaned up the dishes quickly and she went back to the diner for a few hours, leaving me alone in the apartment. Once I heard her get in the elevator, I went into my room and got on my laptop. Sitting on the couch in our living room, I did some research on ordering a copy of a birth certificate. I figured I could probably order one through the mail and have it sent to Megan's address. Nope. Not that easy. In California, only a person 18 years or older can order a copy of their birth certificate. The only other person who can order one is the parent of a minor. Great. There was no way for me to get my birth certificate.

I closed the browser window and then quickly opened it again. I figured I had better delete the search history before my mom saw it. She rarely looked at my laptop as she had her own computer, but you never know and I definitely did not want her to know what I was looking at. If I really was Emily Miller, then I needed to figure that out without her knowing what I was up to. I thought about the two articles hidden inside the book. Maybe that wasn't the best hiding place. I couldn't give them to Megan, though. Her mom was notorious for snooping in her room. I looked around my small room. There really weren't many places for me to hide things. All I had was a bed, desk, and bookshelf. My closet was pretty tiny too. I kept the articles in the book for now. It's not like my mom would borrow one of my books to read.

That night I had a really hard time sleeping again. I just could not get this idea out of my mind that maybe I was not who I thought I was. I couldn't get my birth certificate. There just wasn't a way around that until I turned 18, and that was a long time away. No way was I going to wait almost 5 years to solve this mystery. I had to know now. Was I really someone else? Is there another family still searching for me nearly a decade later? How could I learn the truth, and could I do it without my mom finding out? I had a feeling I wouldn't find the answers to my questions by searching online. I lived in Colorado. That was pretty far from Chicago where Emily's family lived. After a lot of tossing and turning, I finally came up with a plan. I had to go to Chicago. I would go to the police and tell them what I suspected. Since it was such a huge case, I bet they would be glad to help me. It was going to be pretty hard to pull off without some major help. How was I supposed to get to Chicago without my mom knowing? I wasn't allowed to leave the apartment without her. I had no idea how I could leave the state without her finding out. Since Chicago was pretty far away, I wasn't sure how I would get there. I couldn't take a plane. That would cost a lot of money, but maybe there was a bus or a train. I went online to do some research and figured out what I needed to do. The problem was, no way could I pull it off alone. I needed some help, and I knew the one person I could count on-Megan. I might be book smart, but she was street smart. Once I told her my plan, she could help me figure out the details. She also was really good at keeping secrets, which would come in handy because once it was discovered that I wasn't home for a period of time, my mom would look for me at her place first, and if I wasn't there, both her mom and mine would ask questions. I needed Megan to promise me she would not give me up no matter how hard the moms pushed.

I walked over to the bookshelf, pulled out the articles again and looked at the age progression photo. I walked over to my mirror, stood close to it, and held the tiny picture up next to my face and looked at it, wishing it was bigger. I touched my scar as I thought about the real possibility that I wasn't Emma McKay, and that my mom wasn't my mom. I couldn't wait to sit down with Megan alone and tell her my plan. I just hoped she wouldn't think it was too crazy or impossible.

***

Saturday afternoon, I finally had the courage to talk with Megan about my plan. As usual, we were hanging in my room since my mom was at work for a few hours, so we had the place to ourselves. After I told her I couldn't order my birth certificate for five more years, her face fell, but then I told her what I was planning.

I took a deep, calming breath and got ready for her reaction. Somehow I knew she was going to freak out, but I had to confide in someone and she was my only friend, and I hoped I could trust her. I had to. I had no choice. I needed a partner in crime for what I was about to suggest. I looked at her and then spoke in a calm voice.

"I'm going to wait until she's at work and run away to Chicago," I said. Megan gasped, and I continued. "I did some research online last night when I couldn't sleep. A round trip train ticket from Denver to Chicago is $200. I figure I can pack some food to bring with me. It's a flexible ticket, so I figure I can go there and spend a few days to see if I can find out anything and then come back once I do. It's not like I can find out anything more online. I need to go there. Maybe I will even find out where Emily's family lives and I can spy on them or learn more about them."

Chapter 6

Megan stared at me in disbelief. "You can't be serious! You are going to just take off, not leave a note or anything, and travel by yourself across the country? What if something happens to you? Your mom is going to freak out!"

Even as Megan said those words to me, I knew I had no choice. Sure, I could continue to look for stories online about Emily Miller's disappearance and suspected kidnapping to see if I could learn more than I already had, but what was the point? Doing that wouldn't tell me the one thing I really wanted to know, and that was what if I was really someone else? I knew running away to Chicago was risky. Naturally, my mom would freak out and she might call the police, but I was pretty sure she would have absolutely no idea where I had gone. Plus, if I was right, and she had stolen me, then no way would she call the police. If she did, a current picture and description of me would get out locally and maybe nationwide, and someone might think I looked like a missing girl. The newspaper had already run stories online with an age progression photo that looked just like me. What if Megan's mom saw the story online and wondered? She was pretty nosey. She might even call the police. Some neighbor who had seen me in the building with my mom might see the story and think I resembled the missing girl and call. I had to take matters into my own hands before that happened. I needed to get to Chicago and see the police.

The only problem was I didn't have the money for a train ticket or anything else I might need, and I didn't have a way to get any. I said as much to Megan, who didn't seem as concerned about that as I was.

"I've got the money," she said. "The only problem is most of it's in the bank. I have $75 in my room. I was supposed to take it to the bank, but I haven't yet. It's from a couple of babysitting jobs. But that's $125 less than you need. I have plenty in my account, but..."

"Does your mom look at your account?" I asked.

"Not usually," she said. "I really just put money in. I only took out money once before and that was when I bought my iPod and my mom knew I was going to do that. Anyway, as long as I don't take out a crazy amount, I don't think the bank would tell her."

We sat quietly for several minutes without talking. Finally, Megan broke the silence. "I wonder if the bus is cheaper? But it would take you longer to get to Chicago, which could be a problem."

Grabbing her laptop, she sat down on the bed next to me and opened up a new browser window and began typing. "It's only $25 cheaper, so I don't think it's worth it. Go by train. I can get money out of the bank Monday after school and we'll take the bus to the train station downtown and buy your ticket. You are planning on coming back, right?"

"Of course," I said. "What do you think I'm going to do? Run off to Chicago and never come back?"

"I don't know. I guess I hadn't thought about it. Have you even thought about what you're going to do once you get there? I mean, are you going to just walk up and ring some strange couple's doorbell and tell them you think you might be their missing daughter? That could really freak them out! They might think you're some crazy person or it's a prank."

Sighing, I realized she was right. The only plan I had was to get myself to Chicago without my mom finding out. I had not thought about anything beyond that. I didn't even know where the family lived except it was in Chicago, which was a big city like Denver. Megan was right, though. I couldn't just walk up and ring some stranger's doorbell. What if I was wrong, and I really was not their missing daughter, but just some random kid who looked like her? But even as I thought that, I knew that probably wasn't true. What were the odds that two girls would be the same age and look practically identical right down to a scar over the same eyebrow? I think in my mind I was already thinking of myself as Emily. I just needed to confirm it.

"The police," Megan said, interrupting my thoughts. "Maybe when you get to Chicago, you can go to a police station and tell someone what you suspect. Bring the articles with you and tell them that you think you're really Emily. Maybe they could do one of those DNA tests like they do in TV shows."

I stared at her. I pictured myself getting off the train in Chicago and finding the nearest police station, walking in there, and telling them that I might be a missing girl they had been looking for. Did missing people just walk into police stations randomly in real life?

"So I'm just supposed to go in there and tell them, 'hey, I believe I was taken away from a family here in Chicago when I was 3.' Is that what you're suggesting? That's crazy! They are going to think I am insane."

"No crazier than when you ring some stranger's doorbell and tell them you think you're their long-lost daughter who was kidnapped a decade ago! If you can even find where they live."

"Well, I really didn't think this out very well. If I go to the police, then my mom definitely will find out where I'm at, unless I don't tell them my full name. I could just tell them about finding the article in my mom's desk and seeing the photo, but then they'll probably ask who my mom is, where I live, and many personal questions. I guess I can be evasive and see if they'll help me. That's all I can do."

In the end, we both agreed on the plan. Monday afternoon, Megan would walk over to the bank after school and take out the money. Then she'd come and get me and we'd take the bus downtown and buy a round-trip ticket to Chicago for that Friday afternoon since I knew my mom was working then. I'd take the bus downtown to the train station and get myself to Chicago by late afternoon on Saturday. Megan also suggested we buy a burner phone and leave mine turned off with her, just in case my mom texted or called me. Knowing her, she could probably trace my phone, so Megan's idea was a good one. With a plan in place, I was ready to answer the question that had been on my mind since I found the newspaper article: Was I really Emily Ann Miller?

CHAPTER 7

I was a little scared to travel alone across the country, but I knew I had to go. I just could not wait several years to find the truth out, and if I was Emily, didn't my parents deserve to know I was alive? Didn't they deserve to have me back in their lives? What about my sisters? It's likely that they were aware of their sister's absence. The family was clearly still looking for me. But at the same time, what about the woman I had assumed was my mom all of these years? I had to do what I knew had to be done, even if it meant hurting her. I was really worried about pulling off the plan without being caught. I was determined to discover the truth about myself, and I would let nothing stop me. All I could do was pray that my plan would be successful.

My mom was working on Monday night. I held the train ticket Megan and I purchased earlier that day. She had a smooth trip to the bank. No one had even asked her why she was taking out so much money. She withdrew $200 and combined it with the $75 she had at home, giving me some extra money in case I needed it for bus fare or food. For my train ride from Denver to Chicago, I planned to pack light - just a few clothes, food, and my laptop and books for entertainment. I'd already looked at the map. It was going to be a long ride, but hopefully it would get me the answers I needed. With my mom working Friday night until 10, and my train leaving at 5, I was only going to get a few hours head start. I knew she'd panic when she came home and I wasn't home, especially that late at night. It's likely that she would reach out to Megan first, then try to contact me through text or call, but she wouldn't be able to reach me since my phone would be concealed and powered off. Megan had even figured out how to disable tracking so my mom wouldn't see the phone was nearby but I wasn't. I was hoping that Megan wouldn't break under the strain of my mom and possibly her mom grilling her about my whereabouts.

Time seemed to drag the next four days. While I tried my best to act normal, engaging in schoolwork, chatting with my mom, and spending time with Megan, my thoughts were consumed by Friday and my impending trip to Chicago. Would I be able to pull it off? Megan's ability to keep secrets was impressive, but she might break once my mom and her mom sat her down and demanded to tell them if she knew anything. Megan was supposed to pretend to be completely surprised and claim she had no clue about my disappearance. My plan was to bring both newspaper articles and my laptop. I couldn't leave it behind as I knew my mom would search it for clues. Although I deleted my search history, I remained anxious that she could find out about my online activity, including searching for news articles about a missing girl in Chicago and checking train ticket prices. I just couldn't risk leaving it behind. Besides, I might need it.

My mom observed, "You're being rather quiet tonight," as we enjoyed a rare dinner out on Thursday, given our tight budget. In a booth at a Chinese restaurant we both enjoyed, we were seated together. Before responding to her, I took a bite of brown rice with my fork.

"I'm fine, just enjoying my orange chicken. It's really good. Thanks so much for suggesting we go out to dinner tonight. It's a nice treat."

"It is a nice treat," she agreed. "We haven't eaten out in ages, and since my tips have been pretty good this week, I thought we could treat ourselves. What's been going on with you lately? I feel like we haven't really been talking as much as usual."

It was my mistake. I was consumed by my obsession to uncover the truth about my potential connection to the missing girl. I spent hours with Megan and scoured the internet for any additional details on the case. Despite not seeing any new stories posted, I continued searching. I wanted to have as much information as possible before I made the trip to Chicago.

"You've been hanging out with Megan a lot these days," she said, reading my thoughts. "I'm glad the two of you are such great friends." Yes, Megan had been a great friend, even better than I had expected. Not only had she and I spent hours together every week just hanging out discovering shared interests, but now we shared a secret too. Over the past few days as we had come up with our plan for me to discover the truth about my identity, we had become even closer. We were now co-conspirators in a plan to solve a mystery. Our plan was risky, but there was no choice. No matter the risk, I needed to discover the truth.

I spent Friday afternoon anxiously pacing the small apartment, fearful that my mom would forget something and return. After I was certain it wasn't going to occur, I hurried to my bedroom and grabbed the backpack I had already packed and stashed under the bed shortly after Megan and I came up with our plan. I made sure the bus and train tickets were inside before grabbing my laptop. I grabbed the large crossbody bag I'd borrowed from Megan, stuck the laptop and the tickets in it, picked up the backpack, also borrowed, and looked around the bedroom, wondering if I'd ever return. If I went to Chicago and the police refused to let me go, what would happen? Maybe they'd hold me and keep me there until they figured out if I was telling the truth or pulling a prank. Figuring I had wasted enough time, I quickly left the apartment, locking the door behind me and not looking back as I rushed down the stairs and outside to catch a bus.

I sat by the window on the train to Chicago, hoping for an empty seat next to me. The one thing I absolutely didn't want was to engage in a conversation with a stranger, particularly one who could recall encountering a scared teenage girl traveling by herself. Luckily my prayers were answered and I found myself in a fairly empty train car as we began the long journey to Chicago.

With nerves kicking in, I gazed out the window, observing the unfamiliar scenery, pondering what awaited me. Would I learn the answer to the question that had haunted me since finding those newspaper articles, or would my plan be exposed before I arrived in Chicago? The time was now 10 p.m. I had been gone for 5 hours and my mom would be coming home from work soon. When she got there, she would find an apartment that was completely empty. Without a doubt, she would panic and rush to Megan's apartment, hoping to find me there. Then what would happen? I had pictured she'd call the police and file a missing person report, but now I wondered if she would. If I was right and she had kidnapped me decades ago, would she really want to get the police involved? Since my mom didn't have any photos of me, she would provide them with a detailed description and the police might create a sketch. I wondered if Amber Alerts were just for kidnapped kids or if the police might issue one for a suspected runaway too.

Needing to distract myself, I opened my book and began to read. I had sent a quick text to Megan, but she hadn't responded except for a fingers crossed emoji. All I could do was hope that she would not crack under the pressure of her mom and mine demanding she tell them if she knew anything about my sudden disappearance if they decided to question her. My stomach was in knots as I thought about what might be happening at home.

***

Meanwhile, Megan sat in the chair, trying not to appear nervous. All evening since she'd gone to the bus station with Emma, she'd been waiting for this moment. It was up to her to keep it together and keep Emma's mom off her trail as long as possible. She had to play dumb and pretend to know nothing. Most importantly she had to make sure no one got the police involved. That would end things real quick.

" I told you. I don't know anything," Megan said, trying to look worried as she faced her mom and Emma's mom. It was 10:30 at night and the trio had been sitting around the kitchen table for 15 minutes, ever since Emma's mom had knocked on the door after coming home from work and finding the apartment empty and her daughter gone. Megan had expected it. Still, when the knock came, Megan, who had been laying on her bed reading a book, had jumped. It was showtime. Time to stall Emma's mom as much as possible and hope she didn't call the police. Emma's train wasn't due to arrive in Chicago until late Saturday afternoon and she needed as much of a head start from any search for her as possible. Megan knew the chance of Emma's mom calling the police might be slim considering what Emma suspected she had done, but Megan's mom might convince her otherwise or even call the police herself.

Chapter 8

As the two mothers talked, Megan listened, remembering the events of the afternoon. Before Emma had left, Megan had met her at the bottom of the stairs as planned. It was easy because her mom wasn't home from work yet, so they'd been able to do one last thing: change Emma's appearance, just in case her mom called the police and they released an Amber Alert with her photo and description. They had agreed she needed to look as different as possible. They went upstairs into Megan's bathroom. Using a pair of scissors, Megan gathered Emma's hair into a long ponytail and got ready to cut it.

"Are you sure about this?" Emma had asked nervously. "It's just hair, but..." said.

Megan had been adamant. "I know you love your hair Emma, but we have to change your appearance as much as possible. If your mom goes to the police, she might have a photo or at least she'll have a description. You can't match it," she said as she quickly snipped off the ponytail right past Emma's shoulder and stepped back to admire her handiwork as Emma removed the band from her hair. "Perfect. a little uneven, but it works. Now for some color," she said putting on a pair of plastic gloves.

An hour later, Emma stood in front of the mirror stunned.

Gone was her long dark brown hair. Megan had first bleached my hair then dyed it a silver blond. That had taken a while, but thanks to Megan watching some YouTube videos, it turned out perfectly. Dark purple highlights completed my new look. Staring at myself in the mirror, I was pleased I looked older too, which was another bonus. No one would think it was weird I was traveling alone. Most importantly I looked nothing like me. IF my mom, or more likely Megan's mom called the police, they'd be looking for a girl with long dark hair. The one staring into the mirror had shorter, choppy silver and purple hair. I even had some of Megan's clothes to wear and a floppy hat to help hide my face a bit since I couldn't change that.

"This is amazing. I look like a completely different girl," I said, still unable to believe it. "I know you said we'd change my appearance, but this is fantastic. No way will anyone recognize me if they are looking for me."

"That was the idea. Now we'd better go," Megan said, giving her a quick hug. "I will walk with you to the bus stop and then I'm going to head home and be ready in case the moms get suspicious. I will hold them off as long as I can. Text me, but I may not answer right away. My mom will watch me like a hawk. She might even take my phone, so stick to texting. No calls unless absolutely necessary and hang up if she picks up. You're in my phone contacts as Destiny."

"Destiny?" I laughed because somehow it fit. We walked down the block to the bus stop. I gave her another quick hug as the bus that would take me to the train station pulled up and I climbed aboard, not knowing what awaited me.

***

Late that evening, Megan had sat in her room watching TV. There was a knock at the door and she froze. Seconds later, her mom called out. "Megan, come here please."

She walked into the living room, knowing already Ms. McKay would be there and she was, not sitting in a chair, but standing there looking at me.

"Megan," my mom said. "I don't want to upset you, but Emma isn't home. You don't know where she is, do you?"

"No, why would I know? We were going to hang out tonight and watch movies, but earlier today she told me she wasn't feeling well so she was going to stay in her apartment and rest while her mom was at work. Is she not there?"

"No she's not, Megan," my mom said. I looked at Ms. McKay and tried to look worried too, even though I knew where Emma was.

"I don't understand it. Where would she be at 10:30 at night?" Ms. McKay said, her voice shaking. "It's not like Emma to just leave the apartment and not leave a note or call me. She's so responsible. Plus, she knows I don't allow her to leave the building."

My mom nodded. "Maybe she left a note and you missed it. Let's all look together."

A few minutes later, the three of us stood in the small apartment where The McKays lived. I volunteered to look in Emma's room. I just wanted to make sure she had not left any clues behind, plus maybe I could keep my mom and hers from looking in it and seeing the missing laptop. No such luck. Just as I was turning to leave, the moms walked in.

"No notes here. I looked everywhere," I said, hoping they would just walk out.

As her mom looked around at the usually neat room, she noticed that the bed was made and everything was in place. Her eyes scanned the room. *Please, please don't notice the missing laptop,* I said to myself.

"Is anything missing?" my mom asked, almost as if she could read my mind. I panicked a bit as Emma's mom looked through her drawers and under her bed. "It doesn't look like it. All of her clothes seem to be here. She doesn't have much since we've moved around a lot." I was quiet, knowing perfectly well Emma didn't have any of her clothes with her. She'd taken some of mine since we wore the same size and I had tons of clothes. She had even worn a pair of my old tennis shoes.

Just as I thought we were done and would leave the bedroom, Emma's mom looked at the desk. "Her laptop's missing," she said. I pretended to help look for it, panicking inside, but trying to stay calm. That her mom had noticed the missing laptop scared me a bit. Now she might suspect that Emma had plans to be gone awhile. Why had Emma insisted on taking it? She deleted the search history so her mom wouldn't find anything, but we both suspected the police might search it, so she chose to take it. She had a burner phone and we could text, but that was risky. My phone was silent and in my pocket. I'd have to look at it secretly, and how many times could I excuse myself to go to the bathroom?

Out of nowhere, my mom said, "Diana, I hate to say it, but maybe we should call the police," interrupting my thoughts. "She must have run away."

"NO!" I yelled and both moms turned to look at me. "I mean, what if she went someplace like the library or a coffee shop and she'll come back and there will be a bunch of cops here? That would be so embarrassing" I said, knowing I had to stall them as long as I could. Inside I was beginning to panic. Stay calm Megan, I told myself. There is no reason for them to suspect anything.

"Maybe Megan's right," Ms. McKay said. "Maybe I'll wait a bit and then call the police if she doesn't come back. I hate to panic for nothing since it doesn't look like anything is missing or has been disturbed. Everything around here closes by 11 anyways. She has been wanting more freedom, so maybe this is her way of getting some."

I breathed a sigh of relief until my mom told Ms. McKay that of course we would wait with her. She even offered to make a pot of coffee. Unbelievable! I mean I could see why my mom said that, but now I found myself trapped! There was nothing to do but sit around and listen to the adults speculate about where Emma was and debate about calling the police. How long could I stall them once coffee shops and diners in the area closed for the night? I was panicking and trying hard not to show it. I was great at keeping secrets, but if my mom and Ms McKay pushed me, (not to mention what would happen if the police got involved), I wasn't so sure I could keep this one. Yet, I knew I had to act clueless as long as possible. Emma was counting on me. The last thing she needed was for me to crack under pressure and get the police on her trail. The police would quickly haul her home and all our plans would be for nothing.

Inside I was panicking more and more. I hoped that any worried look I had would convey my concern for my best friend's safety, rather than indicating that I knew anything. My mom always seemed to suspect when I was lying so I knew I'd better stay as quiet as possible around her and Ms. McKay. Now if the police got involved, I wasn't so sure. I bit my nails, picturing how they would grill me for information. My mom was skilled, but the police were experts at eliciting information from people. What chance did I have against professional interrogators? I just had to stay strong and say as little as possible, and pray that no one called the police.

CHAPTER 9

"I just don't get it," my mom said a little while later as the adults sat sipping coffee. I reluctantly sipped a hot chocolate that Emma's mom had handed to me, despite my protest that I wanted nothing. Trying to stay calm, I listened as the two mothers speculated about where Emma might have gone. I sat there, lost in my thoughts until I heard my name.

"Megan, are you SURE? Emma said nothing to you?" My mom asked, looking right at me.

"Not at all. I told you the last time I saw her was this afternoon. Yesterday we hung out and talked a bit after I got home from school. Then I practiced for my violin lesson and came home, did my homework, and we had dinner. I haven't talked to her since then except for a few minutes after school. I went to the library to drop off a book I'd finished, came home and did my homework. We got a ton today." I tried to look as calm as possible, but it was getting hard with both moms staring at me and asking me questions. I felt like I was being grilled and I didn't like it one bit.

11:00... 11:15... 11:30... I watched the time pass on the clock on the microwave, knowing something would happen soon. I wondered how far Emma was. It was an 18 hour trip, and she was only six hours into it. By my calculations, she was somewhere in Kansas. Definitely not far enough. I knew I could only stall them for so long. Before long, my mom would call the police herself, no matter what Emma's mom said. Maybe we should have had Emma leave sooner, get an earlier start, but that hadn't been possible. There was just one train.

Sure enough. 11:45 came. My mom looked at the clock and then at Ms. McKay. "I think we need to call the police, Diana. Everything closed almost an hour ago and there's still no sign of Emma. Do you have any idea where she might have gone? Any relatives or friends we should try calling?" I knew I was Emma's only friend. I wasn't sure if she stayed in touch with anybody from other places she'd lived and she'd told me they had no family. It was just her and her mom. I was sure about that.

"There is my sister in Arizona," Ms. McKay said, to my surprise. "I don't know if she'd go there or how she'd even get there, but I can call her, but she has no money that I know of." I sat in silence, wondering about this 'aunt' in Arizona my best friend had never mentioned since her mom claimed she had no siblings.

Ms. McKay left the room, and we heard her whispering on the phone in the bedroom. A few minutes later, she was back, shaking her head. "My sister and I aren't very close," she said. "She hasn't heard from Emma, but said she'd be in touch if she does."

I knew right then there was no aunt. Ms. McKay was obviously hiding something. Her "phone call" had been rather brief and even though I only caught snippets of the "conversation," Ms. McKay had appeared remarkably calm for someone whose only child was missing. My mom would have been hysterical on the phone, plus she would have called the police right after checking with my friends. Also, her mom had walked out of the room with the phone when she could have made the phone call within our sight. What was she trying to hide? Why didn't she make the call in front of us? I knew it was a fake call.

My mom, of course, believed her. "We'd better call the police then," she said. Emma's mom nodded. I was quiet, hoping I could hold it together and keep Emma's secret once the police got involved. Emma was counting on me, her best friend, to keep her secret, and I had to do it, no matter what.

***

Less than 10 minutes later, the three of us sat in the tiny living room with the police. I tried to act normally as the two police officers, Detective Lisa Smith and Detective Michael Stone, their notebooks open, wrote what my mom and Ms. McKay were telling them. I had stayed quiet so far, trying to look concerned about my missing friend and not at all aware of where she might be. I thought I was doing a pretty good job until Detective Smith looked at me, her piercing blue eyes staring at me. Uh oh, I thought, the interrogation was about to begin.

"You two girls are close, best friends?" She asked. "I have a daughter about your age and I know she and her best friend tell each other everything. That's how girls are, isn't that right? You tell each other things you might not tell your parents?"

"Yes, Emma and I are best friends. Actually, I'm her only friend because she hasn't lived here long, and she is homeschooled," I began, attempting to stall for a bit, deciding how I should move forward. I wanted to appear helpful and concerned, but I really did not want to give away Emma's secret, even though in my mind I wondered if some secrets were worth sharing and just maybe these detectives could help Emma.

But as quickly as that thought entered my brain, I dismissed it. If Emma was right and she was not who she thought she was, I really had no proof. Emma had taken the newspaper clippings and printouts from her Internet search with her. She had even taken her laptop. Plus, if Ms. McKay was really not her mother, but a kidnapper, did I really want to let her know I knew that? No. Best to keep quiet. Continue acting like a concerned and worried friend. I tried my best to act as if I really wanted to help the police find Emma when really I wanted the opposite.

"We tell each other a ton of stuff, but honestly, she mentioned no reason she would want to run away. She and her mom always seemed happy whenever I'm over here, and that's a lot," I said, forcing a little laugh.

"What kinds of things do you talk about?" Detective Stone asked, his eyes kind. "Anything you can tell us, anything at all, could be helpful."

"I don't know, typical stuff, I guess, TV shows we like, books we've read. I tell her about school and what it's like since she doesn't go. She's homeschooled by her mom, but she and I have been talking about her trying to go to a public school like me next year," I said.

Ms. McKay, who had been rather quiet, said, "Yes, Emma and I talked about it quite a bit and we decided it would be best to continue with the homeschooling. She has always shown quite advanced skills for her age."

The detectives continued to talk with Ms. McKay and my mom listened and I sat there silently studying Ms. McKay. Call me crazy, but she did not look like a mom who was distraught. Sure, she had tears in her eyes as she talked and she sounded upset as she talked, but she was nowhere as hysterical as my mom would have been if I was the one missing. I was definitely more than a bit suspicious. Maybe Emma was right and Ms. McKay was not her mother. I would not sell Emma out and tell the truth about where she was, but if I had to be honest with myself, I was worried about her and wondering if she was doing okay out on her own.

***

Emma was sitting on the train reading a book to pass the time, when a voice called out to her.

"Are you traveling all by yourself?" the older woman sitting across the aisle from me asked, looking at me through her oversized glasses. She was about 60 with short dark hair streaked with gray. She had been reading, but I had seen her glance at me a few times. I figured it was because of my hair. It was pretty noticeable.

"Yeah, I'm going to Chicago to visit my dad for a week. "My parents are divorced, and he spends two weeks with me every summer," I lied.

"That's nice. I'm sure your dad will be so happy to see you," she said, smiling at me. "I have daughters older than you, but I'm not sure I could have put them on a train by themselves at your age. I'm surprised your mom did not have you fly. It's faster."

"The train was my idea," I said. "I thought it sounded like a fun adventure. Despite being 15, I just look young for my age." I just hoped she did not look at me too closely. Even though I had changed my appearance, I was still a girl my age traveling alone from Denver and my mom may have contacted the police by now. There might have even been a description released by them.

The woman looked at me. "That's some crazy hair you have," she said, taking in my silver blonde hair with purple highlights. It definitely made me stand out. I had been all for changing my appearance, but now, after having someone comment on it made me wish we had just bleached it and not added any crazy colors. "You teenagers today," she said, shaking her head.

I proudly mentioned that my mom works as a hairdresser, coming up with that response quickly. "She's always wanting to cut and color my hair. My dad might think this is crazy, though. He's pretty conservative, being a business executive and all." Wow! The lies kept flowing out of me. For someone who had little experience talking with strangers, I thought I was doing a pretty good job until the woman spoke again.

"I just cannot believe your parents let a girl of 15 travel by herself," she said. "My daughters are grown now, but I would have never allowed them to go on a train trip alone at your age," she said. "Chicago's a long trip for such a long girl to make by herself."

"I actually did it last winter at Christmas break," I said. "I'm pretty responsible." I tried to sound confident, but inside I was nervous. I had been hoping to travel solo without anyone noticing me, but this woman not only noticed me, but was striking up a conversation. Didn't she have anything better to do than talk with a teenager?

The woman smiled at me, a nice grandmotherly smile. "Well, being a mother myself, I'm glad I'm headed to Chicago, too. It will be nice to have someone to talk with on the long trip, and I'm sure your mom would appreciate someone keeping an eye out for your safety." To my dismay, the woman picked up a bag of what looked like knitting and took the empty seat next to me. So much for privacy and having the seat to myself.

Great. Now not only had I attracted the attention of a stranger, but she was now insistent on sitting by me and talking with me the entire time. I only hoped I could keep my distance a bit. The last thing I needed was this strange lady to get suspicious about me and alert somebody. I just had to hope that if I stayed quiet and did not engage her in a lot of conversation, she would write me off as a moody teenager. I opened my book and began reading, hoping it would discourage any further conversation, but of course, being an older lady who seemed nosey, it wasn't long before she began talking with me again.

"So what part of the city does your dad live in?" she asked. I had to think quickly because Megan and I didn't research where people might live in the city. In fact, I had only a few pieces of information that might assist me in my search: the address of the park where Emily was abducted and the address of the nearby police station. I knew they were both downtown, but I didn't know what places there were to live, if anywhere near there.

"Actually…" I began, stalling for time, because my dad recently got remarried and he and his wife bought a new place together. So, I'm not sure where in the city it is since he lived somewhere different last year, in Winnetka. You know where the first Home Alone movie was filmed? I'm kind of bummed because he had a really nice place, but really it was too big for him once he and my mom split and she and I moved." I was really proud of myself for coming up with this so quickly. Now I just had to remember to keep my story simple so I could remember what I told her later. It was a long trip to Chicago, and I definitely did not need to make this lady suspect anything was up and that I was anyone but a weird-looking teenage girl traveling to see her divorced dad over winter break.

"That must be hard on you with your parents divorced and your dad getting remarried," the woman said. "By the way, I'm Marie. Marie Davenport," she said.

"Not really," I said, avoiding introducing myself. "They got divorced a few years ago and I've always been really close to my mom since my dad travels for work a lot. It's not like we saw him a lot. Plus, he met my stepmother a few months after my mom and him divorced, so she's been around for a while."

"So many families these days just do not stay together. It's a shame. Now I'm quite a bit older than your parents, but in my time you got married, you stayed married, none of this raising kids in two different households in two different states and shipping your kids across country by themselves for holidays," she said in a tone that made me think she was judging me and my fictional dad. "But of course, who am I to judge what people do these days? It's just me and my husband, Bob, God Rest His Soul, were together for almost 40 years before cancer stole him from me. He died last year when my youngest granddaughter was in 8th grade. Poor man never even saw his baby graduate."

"I'm sorry. That's really sad," I said, meaning it, but I thought that was just a little too much information to share with a complete stranger you just met. Did this woman not have any boundaries? I mean, I was just a kid and here was this lady I had never met before and would never see again, telling me some super personal stuff about her life.

"It was horrible. I just wish he had gone to the doctor much earlier, but that's a man for you. He dismissed all the symptoms until I saw him coughing up blood one day. I dragged him to the doctor myself and lectured him all the way there." (Of course you did, I thought to myself). "By then, it was too late. Stage 4 lung cancer. He was dead in

6 months. Of course, I was lonely, so I moved into a house to be close to my daughters' families.

Okay, this was definitely way more information than I needed to hear. Seriously, this lady needed to have boundaries. I almost wished I had my phone so I could text Megan. She would roll her eyes hearing this old lady go on and on.

"Well, I'd better get back to my book. Required school reading," I said, giving her a small smile.

"Required school reading over break? That is just too much! What is wrong with schools these days making kids do homework over break? You should have fun."

"Well, I go to a fantastic school and I actually like reading, so I don't mind," I said, opening my copy of "To Kill A Mockingbird." I definitely needed to discourage this woman from any further conversation. I turned toward the window and tried to immerse myself in the book, hoping she would find something else to do.

CHAPTER 10

As the train moved slowly towards Chicago, I looked at my watch. It was now the middle of the night. I looked over at my unintended traveling companion, the nosey Marie, who was now fast asleep. I decided to get some sleep myself, even though I was too nervous about what might lie ahead.

It turns out sleeping on a train is really, really hard. My neck hurt from resting it on the back of my balled up hoodie and I had cramps in my lower legs. I looked over at Marie, who was still sleeping. The train would arrive in Chicago late the following afternoon. Being a weekend, I figured there wasn't much I could do. I took out a notebook and thought about writing some notes to myself since Marie was sleeping and couldn't bug me. The last thing I needed was her nosing into my business any more than she had. I definitely wouldn't put it past her to read over my shoulder and see what I was writing. I wished now that I had taken an aisle seat so I could get up and move to a new location, maybe a different car several cars away from Marie, but I had chosen the window seat when the train was empty thinking it would be nice to have the space to myself. Suddenly, I had an idea. I grabbed the backpack my feet had been resting on and carefully set it on the empty seat in front of me. I tucked my notebook back into the crossbody bag I was wearing and slowly climbed over Marie, being careful not to touch her. Once I was in the aisle, I steadied myself on the empty seat in front of me, grabbed the backpack, and scanned the train car. It was pretty empty. As much as I would love to move to another car and ditch Marie, I knew that might look suspicious. I moved to the seat across the aisle, the one she had vacated, and spread out. I placed the backpack on the floor again, laid across the bench, and took out my notebook once again.

I started by writing exactly what I knew from the newspaper articles and online research I had done into Emily Miller's disappearance. Like any excellent researcher, I carefully made detailed notes. Then I turned to a new page and started writing places I could visit to find out more information.

The library! I thought. That's where I needed to go. Maybe there I could find some newspapers from the time Emily disappeared that would give me more information. This plan might actually work.

Feeling exhausted, I put my notebook away and tried to get some rest. It was almost 8:30 in the morning and we wouldn't be arriving in Chicago until 4:30 that afternoon.

"There you are!" Marie's voice broke the silence. "I woke up, and you weren't next to me. I hope my snoring didn't keep you from getting some sleep. Bob used to complain about that for years. I would tell him I didn't snore, but of course he never believed me. He said it was like sleeping next to a foghorn."

Of course, Marie was up and awake and obviously full of energy. I could not take eight hours of her droning on about her late husband, who died too soon, or hear more stories about her kids. I should have moved cars when I'd had the chance and maybe she would not have come looking for me. Now here we were, and I found myself trapped across the aisle from her.

"I was just going to grab some breakfast," she said. "Grab your stuff and join me," she said.

"No thanks, I actually packed some food." I said, trying to discourage her.

"Nonsense, what kind of person would I be if I left a vulnerable young girl alone in a train car when I went off to have some tea and some breakfast? I'd never forgive myself if something happened to you. You never know what kind of harm can come to a young girl traveling by herself. I mean, you know the world nowadays. It's a scary place. There's many bad people out there who are looking to take young girls."

My heart skipped a beat. Did that mean whoever took Emily, possibly my mom, was a bad person? Did she make a terrible choice in a moment and now has to live with it forever, or is she evil? If she had taken me when I was three, why had she kept me for years and raised me like her own daughter?"

Luckily, Marie was too busy talking to notice I had become silent. I heard her drone on and on, saying something about kidnapping young girls and human trafficking. This woman was going to drive me nuts.

"So breakfast, let's go. My treat," she said. "It will make me feel good to take care of you since you're traveling all by yourself."

What could I do, but agree? I grabbed my bag and followed her to the dining car. Before I knew it, we were sitting down, and she was ordering us both breakfast. When I protested I wasn't that hungry, she looked at me, shaking her head. "You girls these days barely eat, always rail thin. My granddaughters, Allison and Elizabeth, are the same way.

They're about your age. Elizabeth actually struggled with an eating disorder a few years ago, but thankfully that's behind us now," she said. Again, with too much information! Did I really need to know these personal details about someone's family, someone I would thankfully never see again after today? I turned away and tried to imagine what was happening back home.

As they walked to the dining car, Marie looked at Destiny. What kind of parents would send a young teen on a train across the country for two days by herself. She supposed they were following the law since the girl was older, but still, it was a long trip without an adult. It was a good thing she was there to make sure nothing would happen to her. She intended to stay nearby at all times, and not let her out of her sight. She might even insist on taking her to her fathers' house. It just wouldn't be right to send her wandering around the city by herself, no matter how capable the girl believed she was.

***

It seemed like we had been at the apartment for hours. While my mom and Ms. McKay talked, I mostly sat there quietly and listened. Thankfully, I had thought to grab my drawing pad and a few pencils as we headed out the door so I had been sitting there sketching, and the adults had been so busy talking that they didn't seem to mind that I was not taking part in their conversation. My mind kept wandering to Emma and what was happening. She was still on her way to Chicago. I was Emma's only friend, and I was sitting there trying to remain calm, while inside I was freaking out about what might happen.

I knew from looking at the clock that Emma was now in Chicago and that she might try to reach me. Several hours before, I had received a text message from her when my mom was in the bathroom. She had apparently met some nosey older woman named Marie who wouldn't leave her alone, but all she had said was that she was arriving in Chicago soon and she was okay. I knew she was going to call me later.

"Megan." My mom's voice caught my attention. "Did you not hear Ms. McKay ask you a question?"

"No, sorry," I said. "I guess I was daydreaming." Both adults looked at me strangely. Since I was usually a chatty girl, I knew they were probably wondering about my unusual behavior. I definitely wasn't acting like myself, but then again, it's not like Ms. McKay had been acting like a mother of a runaway girl should be acting. She was just sitting here talking with my mom like it was any other day, not that the two moms had ever hung out. This was a first for them and I think it was only because I was Emma's friend.

"I was just asking if you could remember anything Emma might have said to you? I know you girls are close, and I'm surprised she did not tell you she was leaving."

"No. I know nothing," I blurted. "I mean, Emma and I are really great friends, but I guess even friends have secrets from each other. I definitely do not know where she is or why she left. Maybe she was unhappy here. I know she was mad that you've been moving around a lot and that you wouldn't let her attend school with me." Great. Now I could not stop talking. I'd better stop before I blurted out something about the newspaper articles Emma had found and showed me or the plan we had made. If I wasn't careful, the whole plan could unravel right before my eyes and if that happened, I knew I would be in deep, deep trouble, more trouble than I had ever been in before and probably not just with the two mothers, but possibly with the police. After all, Emma had run away to another state, and I was an accomplice, since I had helped her make the plan, find the bus and train she had taken, and even given her my money to run away. I was just as guilty as her, if not more so. That thought made me stop talking.

"Maybe you should call the police again, see if there's an update?" My mom suggested, but Ms. McKay shook her head.

"No, No. I'm sure they would call or come by if they had any news. They said they would put out a missing person alert and I'm sure the police are doing everything they can to find her," she said.

"We should call the paper and have them send a reporter out to do a bigger story, really get the word out. I just wish you had a photo of Emma." She looked at me. A news story? Reporters? Oh, this was getting bad quick.

"Megan, go get your phone. I'm sure you must have some photos in it. Maybe we can print one out and give it to the police or the newspaper. Sitting here won't help us find Emma. We need to do something. Go!"

I got up and walked out the door, and headed to our apartment to get my phone. It was sitting on my desk right where I had left it. I looked at the call log. No more calls. I deleted the voicemail Emma had left me. Suddenly, the phone rang. I answered it in a whisper.

"Emma?" I whispered as I sat down on my bed.

"It's me. Can you talk? I excused myself for a minute to use the bathroom. Marie insisted we get a bite to eat."

"Just for a minute. My mom and your mom are in your apartment and they just sent me to get my phone so they can find a photo of you to give to the police."

Emma gasped. "No! You cannot give them a picture of me!"

I sighed. "You have no idea what I'm going through here. Last night, my mom made your mom call the police when she came home and you were not there. The police were there for almost two hours, taking down information and questioning me. Then the paper has a story about you going missing. They think you ran away."

"How's my mom? She must be going crazy!"

"That's the strange thing," I said, still whispering. "Your mom is super calm. She and my mom are chatting over tea like it's a social visit. She doesn't seem at all concerned that you are missing. Oh, and she called your aunt in Arizona last night to see if she had heard from you."

"Aunt? I don't have an aunt. As far as I know, my mom is an only child," Emma said. "Did you hear the call?"

"Not much," I admitted. "She walked into another room to make it, which was a bit strange, and I'm not sure she made a call. It sounded kind of fake and, like I said, she has been super calm about this whole thing. My mom, on the other hand, is freaking out! In fact, I'd better go. They are going to wonder why I'm taking so long."

CHAPTER 11

As we ate breakfast, Marie did most of the talking. Wow! Could that woman talk! I hadn't known her for years, yet I felt like I knew so much about her life and her family. I learned she had 12 grandchildren and everyone in the family was super close. In fact, she babysat for a few of her youngest grandchildren pretty often and would even take them to the park.

"Is that Bessie Coleman Park?" I suddenly asked, remembering that it was the name of the park where Emily had been taken. Marie looked surprised. "It is. Are you familiar with it? You said you aren't from here." I thought quickly. "It's just that my dad has taken me there before, when I was a little kid. Obviously I haven't been there in a long time, but I remember it's an enormous park. Aren't you afraid your grandchildren would get lost there?" I asked. Marie laughed. "I'm not a grandmother that sits on the bench and knits or reads. I like to follow them around as they play at the park, push them on the swings, catch them at the bottom of the slide, that kind of thing." Of course she did. Marie seemed so nice, nosey, but nice. If I was really Emily, it made me sad to think that somewhere out there I had grandparents. I wondered if mine were still alive. What about cousins? I probably had a whole family out there. I got tears in my eyes. Quickly, I wiped them away, but of course Marie noticed.

"Oh no, what's wrong?" she asked. "Are you missing your mom? It's probably so hard to be away from her for a few weeks. I never could understand how parents can divorce, and you live across the country. I cannot believe a judge allowed your mom to move so far from your dad."

My mom. Yeah, I was missing my mom alright and the comfort of our little apartment and Megan, but then I started thinking somewhere out there, my actual family was probably missing me even more and had been for almost 10 years. I was more determined than ever to find out the truth, not just for me, but for them. Then I thought about the woman who, until recently, I had assumed was my mom. Had I not been snooping and found that news article, I would not be sitting here on a train to Chicago, maybe about to change my life forever. That was a pretty scary thought.

I realized Marie was looking at me, almost like she was expecting a response. "Well, actually it was my dad who moved," said, thinking quickly. "He got a job transfer right after the divorce, so he and my mom worked things out so I spend school vacations with him and a few weeks each summer. We talk on the phone a lot too. It's not too bad."

"Hmm...Well I still think parents are better off staying together. My husband and I were married for years. Sure, we may have had problems at times, but we stuck it out. I guess parents these days don't have the same kind of commitment."

I figured it was best not to say anything as Marie seemed to be very critical on this subject. Besides, I really was tired of making up stories. I was starting to wish I had not sat down near her as she was quite nosey.

She and I finished up our meal, and I thanked her. With limited funds, I definitely appreciated her paying for me. I didn't really have a plan for when I got to Chicago and I didn't know how long I would be there. As we settled into our respective seats, I laid against the window with a book up by my face, pretending to read, but really I was thinking. We would be in Chicago soon, and I had absolutely no plan. Yes, I could wander around the city, find a library and do more research. I could even go to the park and see the place where Emily was taken. But how would that help me get information? I did not know. I just knew I had to visit the park. Maybe it would bring back some memories.

As the train continued on to Chicago, I started getting restless. I wondered what was happening back home in Colorado and how Megan was holding up. I sent a quick text to Megan, figuring she wouldn't respond, but she did.

Hey

What's going on there?

I have my phone back, but my mom looked through it first and found one picture I forgot to delete when I was in the apartment.

A picture of me????

Yeah, but it was both of us wearing those floppy hats of mine and we were making silly faces at the camera.. It;s kind of hard to really see your face.

That's good. So the police have a description of me. Anything else?

No. Your mom was pretty calm…a lot calmer than mine, for sure. Mine is freaking out, thinking you ran away. Your mom seems pretty chill.

Weird. Keep me posted. Still on the train.

I shoved my phone in my pocket. This was bad. The police would soon have a photo of me-a bad one at that, but also a description. How long before this hit the news or the Internet? I was thankful to Megan for helping me change my appearance. The silvery blond hair with purple streaks stood out, though. Was it too much? As if reading my thoughts, Marie looked up from her own book. "That hair," she said, shaking her head. "Whatever will your dad say? Has he seen it like that before?" I shook my head. "Last time he saw me it was…" I couldn't say brown. "All purple, bright purple." Marie looked horrified. "It's the thing kids do now. A lot of kids at my school have crazy colored hair." She just shook her head. I knew my hair was crazy, but it was the one thing that just might keep me from being recognized. At least I hoped so. With the police having a photo of me and putting a story in the newspapers, I was worried. What if Megan cracked under pressure? I thought about that and worried that they would catch me and send me home. I hoped Megan could keep my secret.

***

Megan woke up. She had fallen asleep on the couch. Her mom and Ms. McKay were sitting at the table, drinking coffee and whispering. She kept her eyes closed and listened to their conversation.

"This is so unlike Emma," Ms. McKay was saying. "I do not know where she would go."

"Does she have any friends in Denver she would try to go see?" my mom asked. Ms. McKay shook her head, explaining they had only lived there a few months and Emma had met no kids. I knew my mom didn't know how much Emma had moved around, and I thought it was better she didn't. I was glad I hadn't shared.

"Any news?" I asked, trying to sound like a worried friend, even though the only thing I was worried about was Emma getting caught before she could find out anything.

"Not a word," my mom said. "We emailed the ONE photo you had of Emma on your phone," my mom said. "I'm shocked you didn't have more." Oh, there were. It had taken me a bit of time, so when I returned with my phone, I made up a story of how I couldn't find it, as it had fallen under my bed. My room was a big mess, so my story was believable. I'm sure if my mom wasn't focused on helping locate Emma, she would tell me to clean up my room. But, clearly, she had other things on her mind.

"Diana, what about Emma's phone?" my mom asked, and I panicked, remembering that I had turned off the phone and hidden it in MY ROOM in a box in my closet underneath a bunch of stuffed animals I had played with when I was younger, but refused to give up. What if my mom found it? No, it was impossible. Not only had we hidden it very well and turned it off, but I had removed Life 360 so Emma's mom couldn't track her, plus the phone would hopefully run out of batteries soon too.

"Oh, I bet she has it with her," she replied, but she didn't seem too concerned. "I will send her a text and ask where she is." I watched as Diana's mom tapped on the phone keyboard and sent a text I knew would never be read.

"Maybe we should call the police for an update," my mom said, picking up her own phone. I panicked again. It was bad enough the police were now involved, but I certainly didn't want them coming over again and asking more questions. I didn't like how the one detective had stared at me, asking if Emma and I told each other secrets. It's like she knew I knew something I wasn't saying, and the last thing I needed was her coming over again and asking me even more questions, maybe even telling my mom she thought I was hiding something. Then I would really be in trouble. The one time I had lied to my mom about something a few months back, she had laid into me pretty hard and I had gotten grounded for a week. That lie, about where I was going after school, was minor compared to this. I had a feeling I would be in a heap of trouble if she knew the truth about my involvement in Emma leaving.

But my mom didn't make a call. Instead, she turned the phone to show us a local news site, where there was a minor story about a missing 13-year-old girl believed to be a runaway. Great. The story had made it out there, at least locally, and there was also a picture of us - although they had cropped me out. There was a physical description of Emma and the type of clothes she typically wore. Luckily Emma now looked nothing like that, and the clothes she wore: jeans, baggy hoodie, and Converse gym shoes were pretty typical of most teen girls. The only thing that stood out about her was her now silvery blond hair with purple streaks, but of course, that wasn't mentioned in the article. Police were looking for a girl with long dark hair and Emma no longer had that.

I grabbed the phone and skimmed the story. It was pretty brief and gave some basic information. Emma had been missing from the apartment when her mom had returned home from work. Her laptop was missing, but it didn't appear she had taken anything else. Authorities urged people to call the police if they spotted any girl they thought might be Emma and to be especially alert around bus or train stations in case she might try to leave the area. I prayed that no one seeing the story remembered seeing a teen girl traveling alone, even if the girl's description did not match the one the police had put out. The last thing Emma needed was an updated description of a girl with silvery blond hair and purple streaks getting out. People were sure to remember a girl looking like that. I was really glad we had changed her appearance though. We had thought it would give Emma the best chance at a head start if the police got on her trail.

Chapter 12

Emma stared out the window as the city of Chicago came into view. It had been a long trip, and she was exhausted. Sleeping on the train had been difficult. She had tried, but she just hadn't been able to get comfortable for any length of time. Sure, she had grabbed a few hours of sleep here and there, mostly when Marie had dozed off because the woman had not left her alone for a minute. Not only had Emma been dragged off to the dining car for a few meals-paid for by Marie, luckily, but whenever they had been in their seats, Marie had chatted on and on. Apparently, she had been in California visiting a friend, but was heading home where her adult children and young grandchildren lived. She was close with both of her adult daughters. They lived in a part of the city called Slone Park, and she and her husband had bought a house right across the street from one of them. Marie had gone on and on about all the things she did with her young grandchildren, which included going to Bessie Coleman Park. Other than visiting the park and the library, Emma had made little plans. Even Megan had not come up with any ideas other than seeing if maybe she could find out more about Emma's case, see if she could find out where the family lived, and maybe go to the police if she felt brave enough. This last part of the plan made Emma hesitate a bit. IF she was brave enough to walk into a police station, would the officers even believe her or would they think she was some runaway and try to see if she matched a description of any missing girls? That was a scary thought. What if she went there and somehow they thought she looked like a missing girl from Falls Creek and called the police there and sent her back? Then she would be back with her mom, or would she? If she was right and she was really Emily, could she somehow convince the police to do a DNA test before sending her back? They might even call Diana and tell her what Emma was claiming, but more than likely they'd think she was crazy and ship her right back without listening. A police officer might even bring her back.

From her text messages with Megan, Emma knew the police had been to the apartment, because Megan's mom had insisted. The police had interviewed Megan, but she thought she had done a pretty good job of acting clueless. Still, one photo of Emma was out there online along with a new story, and Emma knew she had to be careful no one noticed her and thought she looked like a girl reported missing from a Denver, Colorado suburb. She would make sure to keep the hat on at all times and hide as much of her face as possible.

The conductor announced that Union Station was the next stop. Emma quickly stood up and put her backpack on, and pulled the hat low over her head. She wanted to be one of the first people off the train, and she didn't want Marie trying to find her.

"Destiny...." I stopped as I heard Marie call out my fake name. "I know you're going to see your dad, but this is my phone number just in case no one is home when you get there. You can always call me. I hate that you are in a big city all alone." She handed me a piece of paper, which I took and put in a zipper compartment in my backpack. I could just toss it later. I hurried to the exit, hoping to lose Marie in the crowd. I was afraid she would try to follow me and make sure I got on the right bus. I wouldn't put it past her.

"Wait up, I'm coming." Of course, Marie had noticed my attempt at getting to the exit quickly. Within seconds, she was right behind me. Had she shoved people out of the way to get to me? I wouldn't doubt it. The train came to a stop, and I quickly climbed down the stairs. Marie was right behind me and all up in my business.

"So your dad isn't meeting you here?" She asked, concerned. I shook my head. "Nope, I'm going to hop the bus to his apartment. It's not a big deal. I do it all the time. He's still at work anyway, so I'll let myself in unless my stepmom is home." Wow! The lies just kept coming. For someone who prided herself on being an honest person, I certainly was throwing out a lot of lies, but it's not like I would ever see her again. Once I could get away from her, that is. Then I had an idea.

"I better stop and use the bathroom before I find my bus. It was nice to meet you." I rushed to the nearest bathroom. Luckily, there was an open stall, and I stepped inside and locked the door. The nice thing about bathrooms at large places like train stations is there are so many stalls, so no one really seemed to notice this one was in use for a long time. I glanced at my watch. I figured I would wait 30 minutes before leaving, then glance around quickly to make sure Marie wasn't anywhere in sight before heading out of the station.

Once I stepped outside, I looked around and quickly lost myself in a crowd of people heading in one direction. I pulled up the map on my phone and saw I was heading to the main part of downtown, where all the offices and stores were. Perfect. I could find a Starbucks, grab some coffee, and then figure out where the closest library was. I wanted to get online and see if there were any news stories I hadn't seen yet, but I also figured maybe the library would have some newspapers from the time Emily disappeared that might help me out.

Other than that I had no plan and my mission might take more than a day, I realized. Megan and I had planned this whole thing rather quickly, without thinking it through. I had some money on me, probably enough to eat for a few days, but where would I sleep? I was a kid. Certainly I couldn't check into a local motel even if I had the money, which I didn't. As I followed the crowd of people, I realized Chicago was a lot like Denver. It was really easy to blend in. There were so many people around and no one seemed to notice a young teen girl walking by herself with just a backpack.

I was getting pretty hungry, as it had been hours since I had last eaten. When I spotted a huge Starbucks-the biggest one I had ever seen, I walked inside and joined the line. Several minutes later, I was sitting at a table upstairs in a corner, enjoying a bagel with cream cheese, and a caramel macchiato while I connected to the free wi-Fi and did a few searches. First, I found out that there was a library in the city. It was called The Harold Washington Library, and it was on State Street, not too far from where I was. I pulled up the website. It was huge! It had six stories, and I noticed there was a big computer area on one with a Municipal Research Center that had newspapers. This was perfect! It was open, so I finished up my breakfast and decided I would head over there to do some internet sleuthing. I looked at my watch. It was 10 am in Chicago, so that made it 9 am in Denver. I sent a quick text to Megan.

Made it to the city. Camped out at SBUX.

You okay? You ditch the old lady?

Yeah, I said I had to use the bathroom. Stayed in there for like 30 minutes, but when I came out she was gone.

We're back in my apartment. My mom decided we all needed some sleep. It was a long night.

Any updates?

Nope. My mom really wanted to go to the police station, but your mom kept insisting they would call if there was any news.

Your mom buy that BS?

Not really, but you're not her kid. KWIM? If I were the one missing, she would camp out at the police station until she got some answers.

True story.

Your mom is acting weird.

How so?

She didn't show any concern about her only child not being seen for hours. Then there was the obviously fake call to your aunt you say does not exist.

I have no relatives

So the story she told my mom about maybe you went to visit your favorite cousin couldn't be true?

Cousin??? Yeah, no. I have no aunts, cousins, or any other relatives. My mom was a foster kid.

Weird. Why would she make up a story about an aunt in AZ and your favorite cousin?

No clue. I'm guessing she wants your mom to not look for me. Maybe she figures I will come back.

Maybe. So what are U up to today?

Going to this massive library to do some digging, to see if I can find anything. They have newspapers.

From long ago?

> Hope so. The local papers must have covered a story like that for weeks. It had to be big news.

> Good Luck. Keep me posted.

K

I pulled up Apple maps and typed in the library's name, relieved to see it was a short walk away. I hurried downstairs and, using the map, walked towards the library. Once inside, I headed up to the 5th floor to the Municipal Research Center. All I'd have to do was ask to see some newspapers from the date Emily had disappeared, and some for the weeks following. Easy Peasy.

"Can I help you?" the young woman at the information desk asked.

"Yes, I need to look at some newspapers from the week of June 10, 2014."

"That's a long way back, so we store those on microfilm. Anything in particular you are looking for?

"Local news," I said quickly, wondering what on earth microfilm was. "It's for a school project. We're doing a project on how life has changed over 10 years."

"10 years? Go back further than that. 2014 wasn't that long ago."

"It's a decade thing. You know, look at life from each decade, so I thought I would start there, then look at older ones."

The woman looked at me and shrugged. "Okay. I just need your school ID since you look too young to have a driver's license or state ID."

An ID. That was not something I figured I would need. I thought I could just walk into the library, ask to see some newspapers, pull out my notebook, and do some research. I had to think quickly. Pretending to look for my non-existent school ID, I rummaged through my backpack.

"Oh no! I must have left it on my dresser. Can you just let me use the machine, anyway? I came all the way here from Slone Park," I pleaded, remembering the name of the part of the city where Marie had said she lived. "Please? My notes are due in two days."

The woman sighed.

"I was going to tell you I needed it to make an appointment. Access to the microfilm is by appointment only Monday to Friday during the day." She pulled up something on her computer and frowned.

"It looks like we are all booked until Wednesday afternoon," she said.

"But it's an emergency!" I cried, forgetting for a minute I was in a library. "Sorry," I said in a quieter voice. "It's just that my parents will kill me for putting this off. Is there any way to find out about life in 2014 or events that happened then?"

She looked at me closely, suddenly suspicious. "What exactly are you looking for?" she wondered. "Is there a certain event you want more information about?"

Crap. I had mentioned events. I couldn't tell her the truth, that I was looking for information about a missing toddler from 10 years ago. Why would I need to do that for a school project? Suddenly this seemed like a terrible idea, and I had to get out of here quickly.

"Never mind," I said. "I'll just go find a place to sit and go online and look up some stuff. What's the wi-Fi password?"

She gave me a little piece of paper that told me how to get online. I took the stairs to another floor and found a table in a corner, and pulled out my phone to text Megan.

Big problem. I need an appointment. There are none until Wednesday!

Crap. What now?

No idea. I think I will just go online and see if there are any recent stories. See my mom yet?

Nope, and not mine either. She came in early and I pretended to be asleep so she'd let me be.

Good plan. What if I find nothing? Then what?

I don't know. Should you maybe go to the police?

Now you're talking crazy. What if they connect me to a missing girl from Colorado? You said the story was out there.

In Colorado, but maybe not Chicago?

I'll think about it. Talk later.

K. Stay safe

I put the phone back in my pocket and pulled my laptop out of my backpack. I powered it on and pulled up a new browser window. Then I typed in Missing girl Emily Miller and Chicago. After the page loaded, I scanned to see if there were any recent stories, but there were not. Just the ones I had already found and practically memorized. I was hitting a dead end. Had everything we had done-changing my appearance, the money from Megan, Megan lying to our moms, and me running away all been for nothing? Should I just go back to the train station and take the next train back to Colorado and forget about this whole thing? Was this a wild goose chase, and I was just wasting my time?

CHAPTER 13

As I sat there thinking about my next steps, my stomach growled. It had been hours since I had had breakfast at Starbucks and I needed to find some food. Packing up my stuff quickly, I left the library in search of some cheap eats. Luckily, just down the street was a McDonalds. Definitely not my favorite, but it was cheap. I walked in and scanned the menu. There was a two cheeseburger meal that came with a soft drink and fries for $5. Perfect. That should hold me for a while. After paying for my order, I stood off to the side, waiting for my number to be called. I looked around and noticed a large bulletin board. Out of curiosity, and maybe a bit out of boredom as my food was taking a long time, I began looking at some things on the board. There were signs advertising babysitting services, cleaning services, pictures of lost dogs, and then I saw it. Tacked up right in the middle of the board was a paper flier that said MISSING 10 Years and underneath it were two very familiar pictures of Emily, the same ones from the copy of the newspaper I had folded in my backpack. Instinctively, I reached out and touched the poster.

"It's so sad, isn't it?" a voice asked. I turned and the McDonald's worker placing my tray on the counter was looking at me. "I'm a mom too, and it broke my heart when her parents came in here a few days ago and asked about hanging up a flier, said they were going around to lots of different businesses around here."

"Wow, that is really sad. I bet her parents really miss her," I said, taking a last look at the flier before grabbing my food and heading outside to sit at a table.

Once outside, I sat down and began eating my food. So Emma's parents had been at this very McDonald's just days ago. Did that mean they lived nearby? Or did they select this part of the city to distribute fliers because the park was nearby? Just then, my phone rang. It was Megan.

"Hey, can you talk? It's important."

"Of course, but why are you whispering?"

"Because my mom is in the next room and I don't want her to hear anything. I'm in the bathroom and your mom is here. I put the fan on so no one can hear me hopefully."

"What's up?"

"So apparently the police called your mom awhile ago and she came to see my mom. They told her that since there have been no sightings of you locally, that you must have left the state, so they are putting out a nationwide alert."

"Oh no, this is bad, so very, very bad."

"Relax, it's going to be the same photo I gave them unless your mom has one? Anyway, you look nothing like that girl. We made sure of it."

I touched my silvery blond hair and looked at the purple streaks. "That's for sure, but I'm a teenage girl alone in the city. That might look suspicious to a cop here."

Megan was quiet, then she said, "Just be careful and if you see a cop, keep your distance. I have to go. It's going to look weird that I am in the bathroom for so long. My mom has already been watching me like a hawk. I think she knows I'm hiding something."

We hung up, and I finished my lunch. A nationwide alert was bad, but I just had to stay away from cops. I pulled my hair back into a low ponytail and pulled my hat lower on my head. I needed sunglasses. Then I could see people, but they couldn't see me and it would be harder to see my face. I walked across the street to a Walgreens, grabbed a pair of cheap oversized sunglasses, and paid for them without a word to the cashier. Once outside, I snapped off the tag and put them on. That was better. I decided I would walk over to the park. It was midafternoon and bound to be crowded. I pulled up the directions on Google Maps and began walking that way, keeping an eye out for cops, but all I saw was people out shopping, and as I neared the park, moms and their kids walking, some moms with strollers, some holding the hand of their kids as they walked. Suddenly, I felt tears in my eyes, making me glad I was wearing sunglasses. Had my mom held my hand as we walked to the park? I was guessing she had because, like all moms, she wanted me to be safe, but I wasn't safe because someone had taken me, anyway. I bet she regretted taking me to a huge, busy park like this. Maybe I had begged to go, or maybe she took me all the time because it was a cool park.

As I entered the park, none of the pictures I had seen online prepared me for how big this place was. It was huge! There were large sloping hills and tons of playground equipment. It was a kid's dream park for sure, and it was loud and crazy. I nearly got knocked over by three kids chasing each other. Other kids were on swings, going down slides, and climbing up enormous towers. It was a madhouse. I wondered if it had been like this 10 years before on the day Emma went missing. I bet it had, and I bet it would be hard to keep track of your kid in a place like this.

I sat under a tree, watching and just taking it in. I waited to see if any memories would come to me, and they didn't. I took out my sketchbook and hung out a while and drew while I did some thinking. What were my options here? It was going to be evening soon, and I had spent almost an entire day in Chicago with nothing to show for it, and there was a nationwide alert out for me. How much time did I really have before I either had to give up and go back to Colorado or before a cop saw me and suspected I was a runaway? Would they bring me to a police station and start asking me questions? I had no ID on me, obviously, but would they try to figure out who I was?

After an hour, I left the park and began walking around the city, trying to figure out what to do next, when I heard a man call out to me.

"Yo, you hungry girl?" I ignored him and kept walking, but he began walking with me.

"I'm fine," I said, eager to get away, glancing over my shoulder.

An older black man, dressed in a baseball hat, T-shirt, and jeans, stood there. He definitely wasn't a cop, but could I trust him? He must have sensed my hesitation, because he pointed to a nearby church.

"I'm a volunteer at that church over there. We have a soup kitchen this afternoon to feed the homeless. You're pretty young, but from the looks of you, you're homeless or a runaway."

"I'm not..." I began, but he put up his hand.

"Don't matter, we help all those in need. We get folks of all ages coming in for a hot meal. Come on, no questions asked. Just come sit down, have some food, and relax."

Hot food did sound good, and this was free food, which was even better since I had little money. He walked with me to the church and we headed inside to a large room that was set up with a bunch of tables. People of all ages were sitting at them. Some were older and obviously homeless. Others were younger, and some had kids with them. Maybe they were just poor. At one end of the room, people were in line, waiting for something that smelled amazing. Honestly, I was so hungry, I would eat anything. One volunteer handed me a bowl of piping hot food, and I looked at it. It was chicken and rice. It smelled delicious. At the end of the table, there were some packs of plastic utensils and napkins, along with rolls. I took utensils and a roll and headed to the farthest table. It was by a TV where the news was on. I ate and mindlessly watched the news. Suddenly I gasped, glad that no one sitting by me had noticed. On the TV screen, Emily's toddler picture and the age progression one appeared in the screen's corner as the reporter began talking about a toddler who had been missing for 10 years. Then the screen switched to the same reporter sitting down with a couple. It was Emily's parents.

Reporter: This has to be so hard on your family, year after year, with no sign of your little girl.

Mom (crying): I blame myself. She begged me to go to the park and play. We had been there once before and it was so big. I had worried the whole time we were there, but Emily loved the park, so I took her. She was with her sisters. I was sitting nearby, so I thought they were safe.

Reporter: How have you not given up after 10 years? I imagine it's hard to hold on to hope.

Dad: It is, but deep down, we feel our Emily is out there somewhere. There have been no sightings of her since that day, but we won't give up trying to find her. She would be almost 14 now, and her sisters are 15 and 17. They barely remember her, but they see her pictures every day in our home, and we talk about her and how someday we hope she will come home.

Reporter: If Emily is out there somewhere watching this, what would you say to her?

Mom: Emily, we love you and miss you so much. I know you are out there somewhere, maybe not in Chicago, but somewhere. I want you to know we will never stop looking for you.

Reporter: What if Emily doesn't know who she is?

Dad: I'm sure she doesn't, but somewhere out there is a teenage girl who looks like that picture that is now on fliers all over the city, and news stations all over the U.S. have it. We're hoping that someone, somewhere, thinks the picture looks like someone they know and will call the police, even if they just suspect something. Every tip helps.

I sat there and stared at the TV as the news reporter switched to another story, but I kept thinking about Emily's dad and how he said someone, somewhere, might recognize Emily and call the police. What if Megan's mom saw the news story and made that call? It's not like my mom (If she was my mom) was with her 24/7. It would be easy for her to make a call without anyone knowing.

I had to come clean. I needed to go to the police here in Chicago and tell them who I thought I really was. Then I would let them deal with everything. Maybe it would be like on TV and they would do one of those DNA tests. Yes, that's what would happen, and if my hunch was right, I could be back with my family, maybe as soon as tomorrow, thanks to the police.

I couldn't wait any longer. I stood up and threw out my trash, eager to get to the police station. As I hurried out the door, I yelled "Thanks for dinner," to some random volunteers. I appreciated the hot meal, but I needed to leave, and fast. I now had a plan, but was I being too hasty?

CHAPTER 14

As I left the shelter, I texted Megan. I decided I would run through the plan with her. After all, she was my co-conspirator in all this.

I saw them on TV just now.

You saw who on TV?

Emily's parents. A reporter was doing a story. They showed the pictures and said they are going to show them all over the country on every news station.

Oh wow. That's huge.

You should have seen them. They looked so sad. Her mom was crying. She blames herself for Emily being taken even 10 years later. I can't do this anymore.

Are you coming home, then?

Well the police are looking for me, and I can't really get more information here, unless…

Unless what Emma?

Crazy idea, but what if I go to the police here and show them the newspaper articles and tell them I think I'm really Emily? I can demand they do something, maybe give me one of those DNA tests you see them do on those cop shows.

I don't know Emma. Do you think they'd believe you?

Maybe. I just don't know what to do. I need you to help me decide. After all, you helped me come up with this plan to run away. You know this is all about getting answers.

Emma stood there, staring at her phone. Megan had gone silent. Then the phone rang. It was Megan.

"Go for it," she said. "I think you have to. It's the only way you will find out the truth."

"I know, but why does this feel so scary? Like maybe it's the wrong decision."

"I don't think it is. You need answers and this way you will know the truth. You need to go for it."

I hung up and looked at Apple Maps to find the closest police station. It was about a five-minute walk away. I rushed to it and pushed open the door before I could change my mind.

*****

"Can I help you?" the young red-haired woman at the front desk asked, looking me up and down. She seemed surprised to have a teenager standing before her. I'm sure I looked pretty grubby after a few days of travel and no shower with my hair pulled back in a messy ponytail and wearing a baggy hoodie, jeans and a hat, backpack slung over my shoulder.

"Um, I need to talk with someone," I stammered, feeling really nervous and wondering if maybe I had made the wrong decision coming here. Why didn't Megan and I plan what I would say?

"You need to talk with someone," she stated. "About what?"

"Uh, I would rather not say. Can I please just talk to someone?'

"Look here," the woman said, sounding irritated. She crossed her arms and looked at me. "This is a police station. I am busy here. I don't have time for games. Tell me what this is about so I can get you to the right person. I'm just a receptionist, and as you can see, I'm quite busy." She waved a hand at a pile of papers on her desk.

I took a deep breath and tried to calm myself. Okay Emma, I told myself, you can do this. This woman will get you to the right person. You just have to tell her why you are here.

"Well?" she said in a more irritated tone. "I can't help you if you don't tell me what you need. Kids these days..." She turned to the papers and picked one up.

"Wait," I said. "Okay, so I'm here because I think I have some information about a case, a missing person case."

The woman put down the paper and looked at me with interest. "A missing person case? Which one, so I can get you to the right detective?"

"One from 10 years ago," I said, trying to sound confident even though I was shaking inside. I was feeling terrified at this moment. What if this woman, this gatekeeper of sorts, thought I was a crazy person and didn't even call a detective, but sent me away?

"10 years ago?" she said. "What were you about 5 then? How would you have any information about a case from 10 years ago? What's your name?" She grabbed a notepad and a pen.

"Do I have to give it? The flier said tips could be anonymous," I said, remembering something I had read at the bottom of the flier I had seen at McDonalds.

"That's for phone in tips," the woman said, clearly annoyed she had to explain this to me. "Fine, no name. What case are you talking about? This is a big city and there are a lot of missing people."

I hesitated. Should I be vague or give Emily's name? I was vague. "A missing girl who disappeared when she was three years old."

"A missing three-year-old from 10 years ago and YOU have information about her?"

"I think so, yes. It might help the police solve the case."

The woman looked at me again, but this time she looked curious, maybe a bit intrigued, like she was wondering if maybe I was about to help the police crack a big case. "Which case?" she asked again? "Do you know the girl's name?"

"Do I have to give that?" I asked, wanting to not say anything more. After all, this woman was a receptionist, not a detective. She couldn't do anything to help me. I wished I had thought this through a bit more. How stupid of me to think that I could just walk into a police station and talk to a detective without having to go through someone else.

"It would certainly help," she said. "Like I said, lots of missing people in this city and lots of them are kids."

"Unsolved for 10 years?"

"Unsolved for many more years than that," she said, pointing to a huge bulletin board with fliers. Sure enough, the fliers covered the board. "That's not even a third of them. We have so many missing people that we have to rotate the fliers every week. These are just the hottest cases."

I walked over to the board and pointed to a flier. "This case," I said, looking at her. "Emily Ann Miller, taken from a park here in Chicago almost 10 years ago. I want to talk to a detective about this case."

"You want to talk with a detective about that case?" She laughed. "You and every money-hungry person out there." Ever since they announced there was a huge reward for new information that would lead to the case being solved, it has been a revolving door of people with 'information', she said, using her fingers to put air quotes around the word information.

"A reward?" That was news to me, but it made sense. "I don't care about that. I just want to tell the detective what I know. Please, let me talk with them."

"Whatever." She shrugged and picked up the phone. I heard her whispering, her hand cupped over the phone. I strained to make out what she was saying. "Missing girl," "Emily Ann Miller," and "runaway" were some words I picked up - and the word crazy.

Okay, so this woman thought I was a crazy runaway. Fine, I could handle that as long as I got to talk with someone, and soon. She hung up the phone and looked at me.

"Detective Stone will talk with you, but I'm going to warn you, he's not one for monkey business, so this had better not be some prank."

"It's not," I said.

"Take a seat," she said, pointing to some chairs. "He will be with you in a few minutes." I walked over to the chairs, took a seat on the one closest to the door, and set my backpack down, prepared to wait for a while. To my surprise, not two minutes later, a tall, gray-haired man with glasses came through the door and stood over me.

"You wanted to talk with me about Emily Ann Miller?" he asked. "Samantha over there says you have some information about the case?"

"I think so, yes."

"Follow me, young lady. This better not be a prank. I don't have time for teenage silliness here. I have important work to do."

"Yes Sir," I said, picking up my backpack and following him to a small office. He motioned for me to come inside and sit at a table. He sat facing me and pulled out a tape recorder.

"You're going to record this?" I asked. "Can't we just talk? I tell you what I know and then you ask questions, and I answer what I can?"

"Look, I don't know who you are, but like I said, we're pretty busy here and I don't have time for games. Now talk."

I paused when he didn't turn off the tape recorder. Then I decided I had better talk. I would get it all out and see what happened. "Okay," I said. "My name is....Wait, do I have to give you that? I would rather not."

"Fine, no name, but tell me why you're here."

I took a deep breath. "Okay, I don't live in Chicago. I'm from...another city. I came here because I think I have some information about a missing girl named Emily Ann Miller."

"What kind of information?" he asked.

I hesitated, then I reached for my backpack and unzipped it. "It would be better if I showed you these first," I said, pulling out the newspaper clippings and placing them on the table between us.

"This is your information? These are news stories. Anyone could have these. Here, I thought you had some information to help with the case. These are clippings anyone could get."

"I do," I said, placing my hand on the tape recorder as he went to turn it off, clearly annoyed with me and the game he assumed I was playing. I could see he wasn't taking me seriously at all.

"Look, since the reward was announced, a lot of crazy people have come in here, but none of them have offered us any useful information. All I have been doing is chasing a bunch of worthless leads"

"But I do," I insisted.

"Then spill it quickly," he said. "Like I said, I don't like people wasting my time, especially a teenager who is probably a runaway."

Okay, here was the big moment. I would tell him what I suspected and once he got over the shock of a missing girl walking into a police station, I would tell him to order a DNA test so he would see I was telling the truth. I opened my mouth to talk, praying he would believe me, and also praying that I was right.

"I'm here because I think I am Emily Ann Miller," I began, and he started laughing at me. That was not what I had expected at all. "It's not a joke. That's why I have these newspaper clippings."

"You have copies of newspaper clippings, "he said. "If I'm not mistaken, you saw the flier, visited the library, researched the case, printed the newspaper stories, and now you're here declaring that you're the missing girl. Like I said, I don't need crazy teenage girls wasting my time."

"I am not crazy, and I have copies because the real one of the first story is at home."

"And where is home?"

"Another city."

"And how did you get here?"

"I can't tell you that."

"What can you tell me then?" he said, irritated."I need something other than a few newspaper stories or copies of stories, and you are telling me you have information."

I took a deep breath to calm myself again as I felt my body shaking inside, partly from nervousness and partly out of fear. I really thought the police would be nice. After all, I wasn't a criminal. I was just a kid. "Okay," I said."Look at the drawing in this article," I said, pointing to the most recent one. "The age progression one."

"That is what we think Emily might look like based on how she looked at age three. It doesn't mean she looks like that now, and it looks nothing like you."

"The scar!" I said. "See, she has a scar above her right eyebrow. I have the same scar." I pulled off my hat and held back my hair, leaning forward to show him.

"So you have a scar," he said, sounding unconvinced.

"It's in the same place. That has to mean something. I mean, what are the odds of two girls the same age who look like each other having a scar in the same place?"

He considered this for a moment, then shook his head. "It's not much to go on," he said. "I still don't think you look much like her."

"It's my hair. It used to be dark brown, but I dyed it. My eyes look similar too," I said, trying to convince him. "I know it's a black-and-white photo, but you see that." Again, I leaned forward to let him get a better look. "Just give me a DNA test, please!"

"Tell you what I will do. I will take a photo of you up close and I will make sure I take one of your eyes and the scar. Then I will show it to Emily's parents."

"Then we do a DNA test?" I asked.

"Not so fast, young lady. I will take the photos, contact her parents, and then we will see about anything else because I'm not convinced there is good evidence you are Emily, and I don't want to get these parents' hopes up. Contrary to what you see on TV, we don't just do DNA tests. We have to have a good reason."

"Just take the photos," I said. A few minutes later, with photos taken with his phone, he told me to sit there and wait. He made the receptionist come babysit me. I guess he wanted to make sure I didn't leave. I wasn't going anywhere, not until he came back and told me that Emily's parents had seen the photo and were convinced that I was their daughter. Then he would regret that he dismissed my claim so quickly, and apologize for not believing me. I smiled smugly as I was looking forward to getting that apology.

But that's not what happened. He came back, didn't even sit down, and looked at me. "Just as I thought. I called them, explained the situation and they were pretty skeptical, but they asked me to email the photos, which I did."

"And?" I asked eagerly.

"Like I said, I had my doubts, but I took photos and sent them anyway, getting these poor parents' hopes up, and they both said you're not Emily."

"Did you mention the scar?"

"Of course I did, and I sent them a close-up photo of your eyes showing it. They insisted you look nothing like their daughter."

I sank into the chair. I was feeling defeated. I had come all this way for nothing. So why did my mom have that newspaper clipping hidden away? It didn't make sense, considering we had lived nowhere near Chicago and didn't know anyone here. I told the detective as much, and then I told him how my mom and I moved every few months, and how she didn't have my birth certificate or any pictures of me as a little kid. I also told him how she didn't allow me to leave our apartment or attend school. I thought I was getting through to him, but his voice got stern.

"Like I said, you're not her. I don't believe it and the parents don't believe it. Enough wasting my time. I don't know who you are or what kind of game you're playing, but you need to go before I try to figure out who you are and where you ran away from."

"Where do I go?" I asked. "I have no place to stay here."

"Then go home. Just get out of my sight," he said. "I better not hear that you are going into any other stations either trying to pull this scam. I'm making a note in the case files as soon as Samantha gets you escorted to the door. I knew this was a huge waste of my time."

I stood up, stunned. Not only had he not believed me, but he was kicking me out into the city, knowing I had no place to go. With no money and only a train ticket home, what was I supposed to do now?

Chapter 15

I stood outside the police station, contemplating what to do next. It was getting late, and I was tired after a long day. I needed sleep, and I needed it badly, but where could I go? I had no money thanks to it being stolen earlier that day when I had pulled out my wallet to see how much I had. Not that the money I brought had been enough to get a hotel room, and I was too young to rent one, anyway. Why hadn't Megan and I thought about this? I guess we were naïve. We had both thought the day I got here, I would go to the police and they would help me, but the detective had dismissed me and kicked me out to the streets, not even caring that I was a kid. I had just been told to go home, but I couldn't, not yet. I had come here for answers and I did not want to leave until I got them. I just didn't know where to turn for help. Maybe I could go back to that church that had served food to people? Didn't a church help people who were homeless? Not that I was homeless, but I needed a place to sleep. I tried to remember where it was and couldn't, but didn't all churches do the same thing? I looked at my phone map and typed in church and saw there was one just a few blocks away. I hurried. It was getting chilly outside, and I only had a hoodie on. I pulled the sleeves over my hands and put the hood up as I walked. I found the church and walked up to the door. As I pulled on the handle, I realized the door was locked. No!!! I walked around and tried to peek in the windows, but the inside was completely dark. Okay, so maybe this church wasn't open, but there had to be another one. I pulled up the map again. There was a church on the next block. Maybe it would be open. I rushed there, hoping that someone would be there to let me in. All I wanted to do was get inside and get warm. I ran up to the closest door and knocked. I waited, and no one came. I peered inside the nearest window and saw a light on, so I knocked even harder, but nobody came. What was I going to do now? Should I just keep trying different churches around the city? Would one be open, or was it possible that churches did not open to let people sleep there when they had nowhere to go?

As I kept walking aimlessly, I eventually found myself back at the park - the same one I had visited shortly after arriving in Chicago earlier that day, the one from which Emily had been abducted many years ago. The tall buildings of the city illuminated the deserted and darkened park. I sat under a tall tree near one of the play structures and looked around. No one was in the park and it looked so peaceful. It was so different from earlier when it had been full of screaming children and barking dogs. I felt calm just looking at it. No one was here and it seemed pretty secluded. I wondered if it was safe for me to be out here alone. Maybe not. After all, this was a pretty big city. I had already had all of my money stolen. All I had was my backpack with my laptop and some clothes, plus my phone. What was going to stop someone from stealing those, too? Then I was absolutely screwed. Before I could stand up and leave to find someplace safer, a voice called out sharply.

"Hey, you! You cannot sleep here!" a tall police officer said.

I looked up at him. He was Hispanic, with short, dark hair. He looked at me with suspicion. For a moment, I worried the police officer I had met earlier that day had put out my description to his fellow officers before kicking me out to the streets, but it didn't seem that this officer recognized me. Still, I knew I had to say something, anything. "I'm not sleeping. I'm just hanging out for a bit," I said. Yeah, that sounded believable.

"Park is closed until 6 am. You need to leave. It's about time you headed home. It's almost 10:30 and the curfew for minors is 11."

"Sorry," I said. "I was at my friend's house and cut through the park and decided to sit here for a bit. Just hang out." Wow, the lies just spilled out of me. I was pretty proud of myself for coming up with that one.

"Well, you can't. A kid your age doesn't belong out here late at night. Lots of dangerous people hang out in the park. It's why we patrol it pretty often. You've got to be careful out here. People get mugged here all the time, even during the daytime."

I wanted to tell him that someone had already mugged me, and it happened not at a deserted park, but on a busy city street, but I decided against it. Why risk him taking me into a station and asking me some questions. In the police station, he might look at me and wonder who I was and why I was really out at night.

"I'm sorry," I said, standing up. "I live pretty close, just over that way." I pointed in a random direction. "My mom's probably wondering where I am about now, anyway." Before he could say anything, I walked away quickly, praying he wouldn't follow me. I didn't dare look back, not wanting to make him any more suspicious than he might be.

After walking for a bit, I glanced quickly over my shoulder and didn't see anyone. I breathed a sigh of relief. He hadn't followed me, but I was still alone in a dark city with no money and no plan. I had left Denver two days earlier with a bit of money and a lot of hope. Now I had neither. I didn't want to go home to my mom-if that really was home, and she was really my mom, but I didn't know what to do. I felt cold and scared. I truly felt all alone in the world. Sitting down in front of a now closed McDonalds, I sobbed. What had I been thinking when Megan and I came up with this crazy idea? We were just a pair of stupid kids. I had run away from the only family I knew, and I had gone on this wild goose chase all because of that stupid newspaper article. I wished now that I had never found it. I would be back home in my warm apartment, maybe curled up on the couch, watching a movie with my mom. I cried even harder. Maybe she wasn't my mom. I would probably never know. Unless I asked her, I wouldn't even know why she had that newspaper article, but did it really matter? She was my mom, or at least I had believed that until recently. Now I wasn't 100% sure. I thought about the newspaper article with Emily's age progression photo. I looked exactly like her, right down to her eyes and her scar. The police officer didn't believe me. He had practically laughed at me, even when I pulled out the newspaper articles, told him how I had found them, and pulled back my hair to reveal my scar. How stupid I was to think that I could run away, pull out a few newspaper articles, and get DNA tested. Stupid girl, I thought. This isn't TV. You're not living in some made for TV movie where you're getting a happy ending. I cried even harder. I didn't know if I was crying for my mom back in Denver, or if I was crying because no one believed me. Honestly, it didn't matter. I had made such a mess of things. If I headed back to Denver, I would never know the truth, and I would spend the rest of my life wondering if I was really Emily. If I went back, my mom would probably ground me until I was 18, and if my mom and Megan's mom found out she had helped me, she would ground her too. They might even ban us from seeing each other again. She was my only friend in the world. I wished she was with me. I pulled out my phone. I needed to hear her voice. It was almost midnight in Denver, but I didn't care. I dialed her number and waited.

"Hello? Emma?" Megan said in a whisper.

"Can you talk? Please," I said through my tears. I had to stop crying so she could understand me. Maybe she could help me figure out what to do.

"Yeah, but I need to keep it down. Hang on." I heard the TV click on and The Big Bang Theory playing in the background. "Sorry, I turned on the TV, so if my mom's listening, hopefully she won't figure out I'm on the phone. She's not saying anything, but I think she's getting more and more suspicious that I know more than I'm letting on. What's going on?"

Quickly, I gave her a recap of my evening, beginning with the police officer not believing me, me wandering around the city trying to find an open church where someone might let me sleep, and me sitting in the deserted park before being confronted by another police officer.

"You went to a park at night??? Are you crazy Emma? Someone could have attacked you or worse! This is getting dangerous."

"I know," I said, beginning to cry again, "I...I just don't know what to do anymore. What were we thinking, having me run away? Here I am stranded in a strange city. I'm cold and I have no money, no place to sleep, and no one who will help me." Between sobs, I continued venting. "I really thought the police would believe me. He laughed at me, accused me of pulling a prank, told me how even Emily's parents saw my picture and said she wasn't me. He wouldn't even do a DNA test and I begged him. I begged him so hard."

Megan was silent, so I continued. "I should just come home and give up. I will not find any answers anyway. It's almost one in the morning. There's not another train to Denver until tomorrow afternoon. I should just see if there's room on it. Then I will be home in a few days. I will probably get grounded forever, but maybe my mom will just be so happy to see me. She has to be worried."

"But then you'll never know," Megan whispered. "Won't that bother you? You might really be someone else, and if you are Emily, her parents will want to know."

"What am I supposed to do? Find out where they live, walk up to the door, ring the doorbell and say, 'Hey, it's me, your long-lost daughter.' I laughed. "As if they would actually believe me. I have no money and I'm dirty from walking around Chicago all day. I haven't showered in days and I feel gross. I wish you were here."

"I don't know what I'd do."

"I wish there was someone who could help me."

"Go back to the police," Megan suggested. "Beg them to help you. Tell them you won't leave until you know the truth. Make them give you a DNA test. Tell them you won't leave without getting it. Push them, or go to another station."

"No way. I'm not going back there. You should have seen the look of anger on that policeman's face. He thinks I'm some kind of prankster. He won't believe me and he definitely won't help me. He even said he was putting my information into the computer so other stations would know what I was up to." I felt defeated. "I wish I knew someone who could help me..." My voice trailed off, then suddenly I had an epiphany. "Marie!" I cried. "I bet she'd help me."

"That nosey old lady from the train?" Megan laughed. "How would you even find her? It's not like you know where she lives."

"That's true, I don't, but she gave me her number. She wrote it on a piece of paper and forced me to take it just in case." I remembered it was shortly before we got to Chicago. "Destiny," she had said. "Just in case no one is home when you get to your dad's place, call me, and I will hang out with you until someone is home to let you in." I had wanted to roll my eyes, but I told myself there was no harm in taking the number. I could have just thrown it in the trash, but I hadn't. I had shoved it in a side zippered part of my backpack, and I had forgotten it until now."

"There's a problem, though. I told her my name was Destiny..." Megan burst out laughing that I had used the fake name she had put in her phone so we could text anonymously. "Okay, laugh all you want, but I didn't want to say Emma. Who knows if she would see the news reports about me and figure out who I was and call the cops? I gave her a fake name and a fake story about taking the train to see my dad for vacation., but if I call her now, I will need to come clean and tell her the truth."

Megan gasped. "The truth? You mean tell her you think you're Emily?"

"Yes. I will call her in a few hours and ask her if I can meet up with her. It's the only thing I can think of right now. I don't know if she will help me, or if she will think I'm crazy, but it's the only thing I can think of. I will show her the newspaper clippings and tell her everything I told the police. Maybe she will believe me, or at least help me figure out a plan."

"It's brilliant," Megan said, surprising me. "From what you said, she's pretty bossy. Maybe she'll march into the police station with you and demand they do something. But don't wait a few hours. Call her now!"

"It's the middle of the night!" I protested. "I can't call up some stranger at this hour!"

"Yes, you can. Nothing is open and who knows what kind of danger you're in if you wander around the city for a few more hours? Just call her. Say you're sorry for waking her, but you're in trouble. She's a grandma. She will help you."

We hung up, and I pulled out the piece of paper and dialed Marie's number before I lost my nerve. "Hello, Marie? It's...Destiny," I said when a sleepy voice said hello. "I'm in trouble."

CHAPTER 16

"Destiny? It's almost two o'clock in the morning," Marie said, suddenly sounding very awake."What's wrong? Were your dad and stepmom not home?

I ignored her question and started crying, thinking about all that had happened today. "I got mugged, and now I'm stranded with no money or a place to stay. I don't know what to do. You said I could call you..."

Marie cut me off. "So they weren't home?" She pressed. "What parents aren't home to let a child in?"

"Um...the kind that weren't expecting me," I replied weakly. I cried again. "I'm cold and I'm scared."

"What do you mean they weren't expecting you?" she demanded. When I heard the anger in her voice, I wondered if calling her had been a mistake. Even though we had spent two days together on a train, we were still strangers, but Megan was right. If anyone could help me, it was Marie. I just had to trust her.

"Where are you?" she asked, her voice softening. I looked up at the street signs on the corner and told her.

"There's a 24 hour diner, probably about a 10-minute walk from where you are. Put this address in your phone, get there ASAP and snag a booth. Order some hot chocolate and wait for me. I should be there in about 20 minutes."

"Okay, thank you," I said, feeling grateful she had not hung up on me, and was willing to come meet me even though it was the middle of the night. After hanging up the phone, I quickly typed the diner's name into the maps app on my phone and quickly began walking there, thinking about what might happen next. Obviously, I had to come clean to Marie and tell her my real name and what I was really doing in Chicago. I wasn't sure how that news would go over or what she would do with the information, but I really had no choice. This was a moment of desperation. I was in a city far from home, with no money and no place to go. I knew I should just go back to Colorado, but a part of me knew it wouldn't do any good. What I wanted more than anything in the world was to solve the mystery of who I was, and going home would not help me do that.

After getting to the diner and settling into a corner booth, I gratefully accepted a mug of steaming hot chocolate from a server and sipped it while clutching the mug nervously while watching the door for Marie's arrival. My heart was pounding because I knew I had to confide in Marie because I needed help badly, but how would she react? Would she think I was lying or playing some kind of game like the police officer had, or would she believe me and want to help me? I could see this going either way honestly. When she walked in a few minutes later, I smiled nervously at her and thanked her for coming. She sat down and slipped off her jacket, placing it on the bench with her purse on top, and looked at me with concern.

"What's wrong Destiny?" she asked. She expressed surprise, actually shock, that I called her at two in the morning. "You said you're in trouble? What exactly is going on?"

I paused. Where should I begin? Should I just blurt out everything and see what she said, or should I be vague with her and let her draw the information out of me? I decided blurting everything out might really freak her out. I twirled a piece of my silvery blond hair around my fingers with one hand and stuck one of my fingernails in my mouth, biting on it gently. Inside, I was shaking as I tried to come up with something to say. I pulled my hand back and started playing with a loose strand on my hoodie as I looked at her. When I spoke, it was in a whisper, even though we were the only ones in the diner other than the server, a cook, and what appeared to be a homeless man drinking coffee on the other side of the diner. The server was chatting with the cook and wasn't paying any attention to us.

"My name isn't Destiny," I said. "It's...Emma." I gave my real name. After all, Emma was a pretty common name. "I gave you a fake name because....well, I didn't think I would ever see you again, and because I thought maybe you might figure out I looked familiar."

She looked puzzled at this. "Familiar? I think I would remember if I had seen someone with your crazy silver and purple hair before."

I laughed. "It is pretty crazy," I said, touching it again. "It used to be brown, but my friend Megan and I bleached it and dyed it then we added purple streaks, so I..." My voice trailed off. I looked down at the table, afraid to look her in the eyes as I continued. "So anyone who would recognize me wouldn't call the police ."

"The police?!" she said in a loud whisper. "You said you were in trouble, but trouble with the police? What are you, 15 or 16? What could you have done?" Then she got it. "You ran away, I'm guessing."

After I nodded, she said, "Your poor parents must be terribly worried about you. You should call them and let them know you're safe."

"I can't," I said. "I just have a mom back in...never mind. It's not important where I came from, but the thing is yeah, my mom is probably really worried, but I don't know if she is really my mom. That's why I ran away. "

Marie looked puzzled. "Your mom might not be your real mom? What kind of nonsense is that?"

I glanced around the diner. It was still empty, and the server was now on the farthest side, refilling the homeless man's coffee cup and chatting with him quietly. The cook was nowhere to be seen.

"She may not be my real mom because my name may not be Emma," I said, reaching into my backpack and pulling out the two newspaper articles and laying them on the table in front of Marie who looked at them and then me in surprise. "This first one I found in a file drawer in my mom's desk when I went looking for something else. It was hidden in a folder behind something else. The other one I printed after finding it online."

"I don't understand, Emma," she said, using my real name. "Why would your mother have a newspaper story about a missing girl? Maybe it's a cousin of yours or some other relative or a friend's child."

"No." I blurted. "We live out west, and I don't have any cousins or any family but my mom, and we have never lived in Chicago or even been there, so I don't think it's anyone my mom knows. I was curious about who this missing girl is, so I looked online and found this other article. Do you notice anything about this picture?" I pointed to Emily's age progression picture and waited.

"It looks like an older version of the little girl," she said. "But what does that have to do with you running away from home?"

"Look closely at the picture," I said, pointing to the scar above Emily's right eye. "The girl has brown hair and brown eyes like me, and this scar right here is just like mine. I think I might be Emily."

She gasped. "What? That's crazy! I remember this case. It happened so long ago when my oldest daughter had young children. For a while, mothers were afraid to take their children to the park, thinking whoever took Emily might take their children. They never found the poor girl. It was big news for a while, but the police have had very few leads."

"That's what they told me when I went to them yesterday," I said. "I sat down with this detective and told him what I just told you. I asked him to give me a DNA test, but he said I was crazy. He accused me of trying to play a prank. I told him it wasn't a prank, and I showed him the scar. He didn't believe me. He took my picture, and he showed it to her parents, but that's it"

"I'm guessing they didn't think you looked like her either," she guessed, and I nodded.

"Nope, and he kicked me out of the police station and told me to go back to wherever I came from. I ended up wandering around the city. I got mugged earlier when someone grabbed my wallet I was holding. It had all the money I had. Luckily, he didn't take my phone that was in my pocket or my backpack. I guess he figured I had nothing worth taking."

"How did you end up still walking around the city in the middle of the night?" she asked. "That's not safe for a teenager of 15 or 16."

"I'm only 13, almost 14," I said. "I passed by a church that was offering free dinner to people. I had some, then I left because I was upset. See, I saw Emily's parents on the news, and it made me sad. I came all this way to tell the police what I suspect and they got mad at me. I just kept walking around the city as I had no money and nowhere to go."

"You poor girl," she said, grasping my hand in her two hands and holding on tight. "I'm so glad you still had my number. I had figured you would throw it out."

"I didn't. I had it shoved in my backpack. When I was talking with my friend Megan back home, and we were trying to figure out what I should do, I remembered I had it. You said I could call if I needed anything, and I need help. I was hoping you would go back to the police and make them listen to me. Tell them I'm not crazy. You're a grownup. They'd probably believe you. I'm just a dumb kid."

"No, I don't think that's the right thing to do, Emma," she said. "I doubt they'd believe an old lady like me, either. You said they showed your picture to Emily's parents?"

"Well, not in person, but the officer emailed it to her dad and both parents apparently looked at it and said I wasn't Emily, that I looked nothing like her. I even had him take a close-up photo of my scar, but they insisted I didn't look like her."

Marie looked at me for a moment. "You sound really convinced, but I definitely understand why the police didn't believe you. This girl got kidnapped almost 10 years ago, and there are lots of girls that age with brown hair and brown eyes. I'm guessing some of them have scars above their eyebrows too. What else makes you think you're Emily?"

I told her about my life back home, leaving out exactly what state I lived in. I just said it had only been my mom and I forever. There were no relatives, and my mom had no friends. Explaining how we moved all the time, sometimes after a few months, I said my mom had no birth certificate for me, but she had her own. I told her how my mom had home schooled me, and how all the baby and childhood pictures of me supposedly had burned up in a fire years ago. I told her about how my mom was extremely overprotective and never allowed me to go anywhere without her. "So you can see why I thought maybe I'm not who I think I am?" I asked, wondering if she would agree with me, and if so, could she help me find out the truth?

CHAPTER 17

Marie sat there staring at me, and for a moment I was worried I had said too much. What if she told me I should just go home and give this up? What if she thought I was completely crazy? What if she turned me into the police as a runaway? I knew I was taking a tremendous risk by telling her all this, but really, I had no choice. I was out of options. Sure, Megan had been a huge help to me with everything until this point, but she was miles away, and there really was nothing she could do except listen to me vent. That was helpful and had certainly kept me from going completely crazy, but what I needed was help to find my family, and if the police wouldn't help me, maybe Marie would. I prayed she would.

"Emma...." Marie was saying. "I've been trying to get your attention for a few minutes. You must be exhausted if you didn't hear me."

"Sorry," I said. I was tired. After all, I had not only been up for more hours than I could remember, but I had spent hours wandering around the city and had not eaten since having dinner at the church, and that had been hours before. My stomach growled. I was so embarrassed.

"You poor girl. I bet you are starving too," Marie said, looking at me with kind eyes. "When did you last eat?" Upon hearing that I had not eaten since late afternoon, she became horrified and shouted for the server. The server came rushing over, and Marie shoved a menu at me and told me to order whatever I wanted. "My treat," she said as I tried to protest. Once the server hurried to the kitchen to place my order, and had brought me another hot chocolate and refilled Marie's coffee cup, she spoke again. "Once you have some food in you, we will come up with a plan."

I hoped the plan involved Marie marching me into the police station and demanding the detective listen to me. I could picture her shoving her way past the receptionist and marching straight into the detective's office and refusing to leave until he not only listened to me, but immediately ordered a DNA test while Marie waited with me. When it came back, I pictured her scolding him, saying he should have believed me from the beginning.

But as I inhaled a stack of the most delicious blueberry pancakes I had ever eaten, that wasn't the plan Marie came up with.

"Obviously, the police are completely useless," she said. "You cannot count on them to do anything. From what you said, that detective laughed at you even after you told him everything. You will not convince him to do anything. It would be a waste of time."

I put down my fork, feeling more defeated than ever. Then I spoke up. "That's why you will come there with me and force him to listen, right? You will demand he do something and not leave until he does. You're a grown up. I bet he will listen to you over a stupid teenager."

She laughed. "That might work. After all, I am a pretty pushy lady. My late husband Bob, God rest his soul, used to say I could talk anyone into anything. I once made a car dealer give us such a good price on a used car that the poor sales associate barely made a commission." She smiled at the memory. "But that's not the right thing to do in this situation. If I go in there all pushy, it won't accomplish anything. They will not listen to some old lady any more than they listened to you. You can't rely on the police, Emma. Rely on yourself and take matters into your own hands."

I finished eating my pancakes. "But everything I have tried has been a disaster," I said, feeling like I was about to cry again. "I couldn't use the library to research anything because I don't have a card and I need a reservation, which I wouldn't be able to get until Wednesday. I have no money and no place to stay. I told my friend Megan I should just go home and give up."

"But then you won't find the information you're looking for," Marie reminded me. "Here's what we're going to do. After I pay the bill, you're coming back to my place and sleeping on my couch. Then, once you have a good night's sleep, I will cook you some breakfast and help you find where your family lives."

"You'd do that for me?" I asked. "But I'm a stranger you barely know. Why would you be so nice to me?"

"Because I'm a grandma and if it was one of my grandchildren who found themselves stranded someplace with no money and no place to go, I would hope someone would do the same for them. I cannot just let you wander around the city alone. It's not safe."

After paying the bill, Maria and I walked to her car, which was parked nearby. As she drove through the deserted city streets toward her house, I felt grateful that our paths had crossed. On the train, her constant questions and over sharing about her life annoyed me when all I wanted was to be left alone, but I felt so smart for taking that piece of paper with her phone number on it. I was glad I hadn't thrown it out because Marie had turned out to be so helpful to me, and I had a feeling she wasn't done. In fact, I figured she wouldn't stop helping me until I found Emily's family and got the answers I desperately needed.

After about 15 minutes, Maria pulled up to a pretty brick house on a quiet street. I unlocked my seat belt, got out of the car, and grabbed my backpack. Silently, I followed her up a few stairs and waited while she unlocked the door. I looked around. The house looked so inviting and warm. A large, overstuffed couch sat on one side of the living room, a coffee table in front of it, and two comfortable looking chairs faced it. On two tall wooden shelves with glass fronts, there were tons of old dishes and teacups. Pictures of children hung all over the walls. It was exactly how a grandmother's house would look, I thought, and it looked so different from those bare apartments where I had lived with my mom for my entire life. This felt like a home.

"It's a mess, isn't it?" Maria said, moving a pile of yarn and something that looked homemade off the couch. "An afghan for my youngest grandson. He's only two, but all of my other grandchildren have one made by me, so I'm finally getting around to making his." She showed me the blue and gray afghan and I reached out and touched it. How lucky these grandchildren were, not only to have parents who loved them but also a grandma. It made me sad to have only had a mom in my life all these years.

Maria set the afghan down in a nearby basket (Of course she had a basket for her projects) and walked down the hall, soon returning with a pillow, a sheet, and a soft blanket. After tucking the sheet around the couch cushions, she set down the pillow and spread out the blanket. "Now you get a good night's sleep. Sleep as long as you want."

***

Maria walked to her own bedroom down the hall. She wished she had a guest room. She could, but really there was no need. Her family lived nearby, and if her grandchildren had a sleepover, they slept on sleeping bags in the living room. Plus she was a huge crafter, so the extra bedroom made a nice craft room. She felt bad about having Emma sleep on the couch, but it was comfortable. She should get to bed herself, but she was feeling restless. She couldn't believe the events that had transpired. She knew she should have stayed with her at the train station, but Emma had walked so quickly it had been hard to keep up. When she had caught up with her, the girl had gone into the bathroom. Marie had waited and waited, but Emma hadn't returned. She was with Marie now though, and Marie didn't intend to let her out of her sight again. Later today, once they both got a good night's sleep, she would help Emma find who she was looking for. After being out of town, she had a lot to do, but she would put all that to the side. This was a real-life mystery, and she could play an important role. If Emma was right, and she did get reunited with her family, there was bound to be newspaper and TV reporters looking to talk, and Marie relished the idea of being the one they talked to. Maybe she would even get to be on to some talk shows with Emma. She fell asleep, imagining herself being interviewed by one of the late night talk show hosts, or maybe Kelly Clarkson would have them on her show.

***

I sat down on the couch as Marie walked down the hall. It was so nice to be left alone, I thought. Removing my hoodie and my shoes, I laid back on the couch. I hadn't slept in so long. I must have been exhausted, because the next thing I knew, the sun was streaming into the room through a large window. For a minute, I was confused. Then I remembered the events of last night and where I was. I got up and walked into the kitchen, where Maria was sitting with a cup of tea.

"Did you sleep well?" she asked, and I nodded. "I made some scrambled eggs. Sit down and I will bring you some with a piece of toast and some fruit."

Before I could protest and say that wasn't necessary, she had a plate of delicious smelling food sitting in front of me. I began eating as she set down an enormous glass of orange juice. Was it rude to pull out my phone at the table? I really wanted to see if I could find my family's address. How did one find an address for someone? Would I just type in their name + address and hope it came up? I wasn't sure as I had never had a reason to look for someone's address before, but then again, the only person I knew other than my mom was Megan, and she lived down the hall from me. Pulling out my phone at the table seemed rude. Maybe Marie would walk away to clean something, and I could take it out, but she sat there, sipping her tea, and making small talk about her garden and her plans for the week, which included lunch with some friends and seeing her grandchildren. I listened politely, all the time wondering if today was the day when I would find out where my family lived. I knew from news stories that they were still in Chicago, but were they in the same house, or had they moved? I finished my food and stood up to take the plate to the sink and rinse it off, as my mom had drilled into me. I didn't want Marie to think that my mom hadn't raised me right. But Maria beat me to it. She took the plate, silverware, and glass to the sink, rinsed them off, put them in the dishwasher, and returned to the table.

"So, are you ready?" She asked. I nodded, feeling nervous, but also a bit excited. With my phone in hand, I launched my web browser. I typed in Nancy Miller + address, but nothing came up. Hmm. I quickly googled 'How to find a person's address' and came upon a site called 411. I typed in the name and came up with a few Nancy Millers in Chicago, but which one was right? Some had phone numbers, but no addresses. Was I supposed to call random strangers on the phone? The thought terrified me.

"You young people and your phones," she said. "I'm guessing you are looking up her name and expecting to find an address."

"There are so many Nancy Millers," I said. "Miller is such a common name, and there have to be at least 15 here in Chicago. None have addresses and a few have phone numbers. I guess I could just start calling them?"

Marie was silent for a few seconds, then she walked over to a little shelf that was under a wall phone. People still had phones in their house? I didn't think that was a thing. My mom and I just had cell phones, and I knew Megan's mom didn't have a phone in her apartment. She returned with a thick book and laid it on the table. "I'm guessing you have never heard of a phone book," she said, opening it up. "This one is from last year. The new one comes out sometime this fall, but this has everyone's number in the city and the nearby suburbs. If your family is still in the same place and has their number listed, it will be in here, along with their address."

"Is it that easy?" I asked. Thinking everything was there, I went straight to the Internet, but it turns out I had to go old school with my search. I scooted my chair closer to Marie's side of the table to check the phone book. Marie opened the book. I noticed some pages were yellow and some were white. Seeing that I was confused, Marie opened to the white pages. I watched as she turned the pages, opening to a page with names beginning with the letter M. She used her finger to scroll down the page, then turned a few pages.

"Ah, yes, here we are. Miller," she said, pushing the book towards me. "Now just look until you see a Sean or Nancy." I quickly scanned the page. I saw there were 12 Sean Millers listed. How was I supposed to know which was the right one, if any of them? I looked closer and two said Sean and Nancy Miller, Okay, so two was better than 11, but which one was the right one? I noticed both had a phone number, and an address listed.

"There are two listings, but do I just guess? It's only two, so I guess maybe I could call them, but what do I say?" I asked her, hoping she would tell me the words to use.

"Call them? No, dear, calling them won't work. This is a situation where you need to go see them in person, get in front of them and tell them what you suspect. Let them look you in the eye."

"Both of them?" I was confused. "I don't even know if either of them is the right family. So I'm just supposed to show up at these two random addresses and tell them I think I'm their missing daughter? They'll think I'm crazy, just like the police did."

"Not both of them," Maria said. She put a receipt that was sitting on the table inside the book to use as a bookmark, then opened another part of the book. "This is a street map of Chicago," she said. I found it fascinating. It was like a printout of Google Maps spread over two pages. She looked back at the listings. "Elm Street. That's right here. Hmm.. not super close to the park. This is downtown." She pulled open her phone and typed in the address in Google Maps. "Just as I thought, it looks like a high-rise apartment building." She showed me the photos. "Now, to me, this doesn't look like a place to raise kids. You said Emily has two sisters?"

"Yes, that's what the news story said. Her mom took the three girls to the park that day. Emily was three. Her sisters were older."

"This is Spruce Street," she said. "It's where the other family lives. It's close to the park." She pulled up the address on her phone, smiled, and showed it to me. I saw a photograph of a two story brick house. Could that be it? Had we found where Emily's family lived, and if so, was I supposed to go knock on their door, and when the parents answered, say 'Hello, I think I'm your long-lost daughter Emily'? In my mind, it sounded like maybe it was a good idea, but could I actually do it? Was I brave enough to go to wherever this house was, ring the doorbell, and announce to whoever answered that I believed I was the long lost Emily Miller?

Chapter 18

I sat there, thinking. Could I do it? It seemed like such a scary step to take. I was not even 14, and suddenly I felt like a scared little girl. Marie must have sensed my fears because she took my hand and squeezed it. Her kind eyes looked at me. She had been so nice and helpful. I felt like I would let her down if I didn't go through with this, but I wasn't feeling very brave at this moment. If I did this, there was no turning back. Whatever happened might change my life forever, not to mention the lives of so many other people.

"You can do brave things, Emma," she said. I shook my head. I wasn't feeling very brave at all. "Yes, Emma. Look at all the brave things you did already. You ran away from the only home you have known and took a train across the country to a city you have never been to where you know no one. When you had no money and no one to turn to, you pulled out my number and called me. Now you have the address of Emily's family. You can't rely on the police to help you, Emma. They already laughed at you. You need to be brave, go to this address and ring the doorbell. Stand in front of whoever answers and tell them you think you are Emily. Don't leave until they listen to you."

"But what if they think I'm crazy?" I asked. "They might yell at me and think I'm playing some sort of joke on them, like the police? I mean, it is pretty crazy that almost 10 years later their long-lost daughter would just suddenly appear at their door."

"They might just think you're crazy, or they might just believe you when you are standing right in front of them looking them in the eyes," she said. "Now, go take a shower and get on some clean clothes. I washed yours when you were sleeping. You certainly didn't bring much with you."

"I tried to travel light," I said. "I figured it would be easiest not to have a lot of stuff with me. Thanks for washing my clothes."

After showering and washing my hair, I ran a comb through my silvery hair, letting it air dry a bit before deciding to pull it back into a French braid. I stared at myself in the mirror, and noticed that with my hair pulled completely off my face, my brown eyes stood out. I wondered if Emily's parents, when standing face to face with me, would see the resemblance I did. I touched the scar above my right eyebrow, wondering how I had really gotten it. I had never questioned the story my mom had told me-that I had fallen and hit the side of our coffee table when I was really little. Why would I? I asked about something I didn't remember and she had told me. It had always been that way with my mom, since it had always been just the two of us. I thought about my mom and wondered what she was doing at that moment. I quickly dressed in jeans and a T-shirt, and sat down on the toilet seat to shoot a quick text to Megan.

Hey, you awake?

Yeah, what's up?

I'm at Marie's house. I spent the night here.

You spent the night at a stranger's house??? OMG! Are you crazy?

She's perfectly harmless. I kind of feel like she's my grandma or something at this point.

She certainly is being nice and helpful

Yep. She thinks I need to go see Emily's parents. We think we know their address now.

There was no response from Megan. I wondered if she was going to think it was a stupid idea, or if she'd agree with Maria. I missed Megan a lot right then, and wished she had run away with me, but I knew she couldn't. Both of us running away would have been suspicious, and someone needed to stay behind and keep the moms from finding out what we had done.

It's a crazy idea, right?

Not completely crazy. It's one thing to see a picture and say it's not their kid, but you'd be standing right in front of them. They might take you seriously.

Or they will think I'm some crazy girl playing a joke

So are you doing it?

I have to.. What choice do I have?

I didn't want to tell you this, but you need to do it soon. I think the moms are onto me

What? We were so careful

My mom was checking her bank balance this morning, and she looked at mine and saw the missing money and freaked out

Seriously?

Yep, I told her I pulled out a bunch to fix my phone, but I think she knows I'm lying. She threatened to tell the police what she had found unless I told her the truth.

Did you???

Of course not. I told her I dropped my phone, and the screen cracked so I had to get it fixed. She knows I'm lying to her. Crap! Need to go.

I sat there wondering what had made Megan cut me off so fast. Suddenly, I was anxious.

***

"Megan," my mom said, walking into my room without knocking. Quickly, I swiped and deleted my text messages with Emma. Good thing as she reached for my phone.

"What?" I asked innocently.

"Just as I thought," she said, looking carefully at my phone. Your screen protector is still on this. You didn't drop your phone and crack the screen."

"It's a new screen protector. I had them replace that," I blurted.

"Megan, you're lying to me. I thought so the other day when you told me you hadn't been in touch with Emma. Now I'm sure of it."

I said nothing as my mom scrolled through text messages and my phone log, knowing she would find nothing.

"I think you're in touch with Emma," she said. I went to speak, and she held up a hand. "I don't want to hear it, Megan Elise. That poor girl's mom is worried sick about her. The police can't find her, and you're sitting here lying to me. You're grounded until further notice and I'm taking your phone." She walked out of my bedroom, not bothering to shut the door,

Great. Now, not only did I have no way to communicate with Emma, but there was no way I could warn her about what happened. I hoped she wouldn't try to text me.

I was still laying on my bed 45 minutes later, staring at the ceiling and trying to figure out how to get my phone back when my door opened.

"Megan. Out here now," my mom said, turning and walking away. I knew that tone of voice. It was her no nonsense, all business, kind of pissed off voice. I better not say a word. I stood up and followed her into the living room. To my surprise, we were not alone. The two detectives from the other night stood there and Emma's mom was sitting in a chair, looking nervous.

"Is this about Emma? Did you find her? Is she alright?" I asked.

"That's what we want to know," Detective Smith said. "Your mom called us. She believes you have been in contact with her, maybe texting her?"

"No," I said. "Emma doesn't even have her phone with her." As soon as those words came, I regretted it. Now it was Detective Lewis who looked at me sharply.

"What do you mean she doesn't have her phone with her?" he asked in a loud voice. He didn't look very kind as he stared at me. "How would you know? I knew you had to know something the other night. You had better speak up this instant."

Terrified, I stood there. The two police officers, my mom and Emma's mom, all looked at me and the first two people were not looking at me nicely. I started thinking I was in a ton of trouble and not just with my mom.

"This is your phone," Detective Smith said. "Your mom already looked through texts and phone calls and found nothing, but we did." I sat there, stunned. Of course they had. They were detectives, after all. "We pulled up the deleted calls and there were none to Emma, but there were a few to and from a girl named Destiny, including a few late at night."

My mom spoke up. I" don't know of any friends she has named Destiny. Megan? Who is she? A friend from school?"

Before I could say anything, Detective Lewis looked at me. "I'll tell you what I think," he said. I noticed Detective Smith standing there watching me. "I think Destiny is actually Emma, and you changed her contact information on your phone, and that the two of you have been in touch with each other. I'm willing to bet there's been a lot of texting. These days, kids don't really call, but they're all about texting. What I don't see are any texts, so I'm guessing you deleted them."

I gulped. I had deleted them, which meant they were gone, right? Would the police be able to pull up the texts between us? If they did, I knew I was in serious, serious trouble. I had lied to the police. This was so bad.

"Like I said, I think you deleted the messages, but luckily for us, it is quite easy to retrieve them. I don't need any fancy technology." I watched as he did something on my phone for a few minutes. "Got it," he said, showing the phone screen to Detective Smith. "Retrieving messages within 30 days is always possible."

I hadn't known that. Suddenly I felt queasy knowing what messages they were going to see. Emma and I had been in constant contact since she had left and we hadn't been careful about what we were saying. I sat down on the couch. My mom sat beside me. "I'm guessing she and Emma have been texting?" she asked Detective Lewis.

"Well, Megan and **DESTINY** have been texting a lot. There are over fifty messages all going back to the day Emma disappeared. Destiny is Emma. I'm sure of it just from glancing at these messages."

He read them, sitting down on the other side of me, while Detective Smith sat in the other chair across from us. As he read, I noticed he jotted notes in a small notebook he carried. What was he writing, anyway?

"Well, it seems Destiny...I mean, Emma took a train to Chicago a few days ago. I'm guessing she boarded one and was out of Denver before anyone noticed she was missing. We'll pull up surveillance cameras from the train station and confirm, but I'm pretty confident that's what she did. We'll be in touch, and Megan, we're taking the phone into evidence. Who knows? Maybe you will get a few texts." He and Detective Smith left without another word..

As soon as they did, my mom turned on me, barely concealing the fury in her voice. "You lied to me and you lied to Emma's mom! What on earth were you thinking?"

"Uh...I...uh....wanted to help Emma. She needed to go to Chicago. It was an emergency."

My mom looked at me puzzled, probably wondering what kind of emergency a 13-year-old girl would have that would require her to go to Chicago secretly. I glanced over at Emma's mom, who had gone completely pale. She stood up without saying a word and rushed out of the room.

***

In the apartment, Diana was pacing nervously. She knew she might make Megan's mom and the police suspicious when she left the room abruptly, but she had to get out of there. She was feeling very anxious and needed to be alone. She hoped they thought she was upset about her daughter running away and so far, that they didn't suspect anything else. Chicago. That was a city she had not thought of in years. She had lived there years ago, but had left for the warmer weather of the west coast, finding Chicago winters too brutal. Why would Emma run away to Chicago of all places? There was no reason for her to go there. For a moment she panicked. Had Emma somehow discovered her secret? No. Diana had been careful. She was sure of it. Maybe Emma had met someone online and ran off to meet them? She didn't really monitor her activity online, but she had heard about other kids doing such things. She sat down and tried to compose herself. There was no reason to think Emma had run off to Chicago for anything but a little adventure. She just had to stay calm, and hope she would be found soon. Then she would move them back to California, or maybe to Montana. That was pretty remote. She could find a little town where they could start over again. Once Emma came home, they would pack up their things and move, and she wouldn't be allowing her contact with her friend either. They needed to move someplace remote where she couldn't meet a lot of kids, and maybe she would cancel Emma's phone.

CHAPTER 19

"Emma? Are you ready yet? It's almost 11:00. We should get going." Marie's voice broke into my thoughts. I realized I had been sitting there staring at my phone, wanting to text Megan and ask her what had happened, but I didn't. I figured her mom noticed her texting. I hoped Megan deleted our messages like she always did. If her mom saw the latest messages, it would be a disaster. She would have the police after me right away, and I might not see Emily's parents.

"I'm ready. Do I look okay?" I asked, feeling very nervous. After all, in a short time, I would stand at the door of Emily's parents and see them face to face. I was quiet as Marie and I got in the car and she began driving through the city. Traffic was heavy, so it was taking a while, which was fine, as it gave me time to think some more. How would Emily's parents react when they opened their door and saw me? Would they see something in me that the police hadn't? They hadn't recognized me as their missing daughter from a photograph, but could they deny it when they saw me in person? Maybe I was delusional and had convinced myself that I was really Emily, when in fact I was just a teenage girl with brown eyes and brown hair who looked like what the police thought she looked like. After all, 10 years was a long time and kids change a lot over the years. I had come too far to turn around now. I needed to know the truth.

"Here we are," Marie said, slowing down the car. She glanced out the passenger side window. "That's the house right there," she said, pointing to a small brick house with a covered porch. It was an older house, obviously built a long time ago. The house had a red-painted door, and two pots of colorful flowers were placed on either side. A swing hung off to one side. It looked like a pleasant house. I had never lived in a house, ever. My mom and I had always rented apartments. I wondered what the house looked like on the inside and wondered if I would even see the inside. Marie passed by the house and pulled into a small parking lot. It was next to the coffee shop.

"Now I'm going to go in, get myself a cup of tea and settle in with this book I'm reading for our next book club, Emma, but my phone will be right next to me. You call me right away if you need me, and I will drive right over. You remember which house it is, right?"

"Yes, that red door makes it stand out, and it's a short walk." Marie opened her door, but I sat there frozen, unable to open my door and get out.

"I...I can't do this," I said. "I feel sick." I gripped the dashboard with my hands and lowered my head toward my knees, feeling Marie's hand on my shoulder.

"Look at me, Emma," she said in a soft voice. I looked up and saw her looking at me kindly. "This is the moment you have been waiting for. You cannot turn back now. Remember what I said about being brave?"

I nodded. "You said I can do brave things, but this is going to be so hard. What do I even say when someone opens the door?"

"Start with hello and go from there," Marie advised. "You're over-thinking this, Emma, and stressing yourself out with all the what ifs. Just walk up to the door, ring the doorbell, and see what happens. I think in the moment you will know the right things to say."

"Thank you," I said, impulsively giving her a hug. "No matter what happens, I know you believe me, and you have been such a help to me. I wouldn't even be here if it weren't for you." I opened the door and stepped out. Marie did the same.

"Now go, brave girl," she said. She turned and walked into the cof-fee shop, leaving me standing in the parking lot. I slung my backpack over one shoulder and walked toward the house slowly. Marie was right. I needed to be brave and do this. All I had to do was walk up the steps to that porch and ring the doorbell.

I was standing in front of the house before I knew it. There was a blue SUV parked in the driveway. I glanced around at the neighbor-hood. It was a pleasant neighborhood with lots of trees. Some houses obviously had little kids living there as I saw tricycles and sandboxes in a few yards, but no kids were outside, but it was almost the middle of the day, so maybe they were inside their houses having lunch. I didn't hear any voices as I approached the porch. I knew I couldn't just hang around as a neighbor might see me and wonder who I was. I needed to do what I came here to do. I climbed the four stairs to the porch and looked at the red door. My hand reached for the doorbell, then I pulled it back. No, I needed to be brave. I could do brave things. It was just me here with no Marie by my side. This was my moment, and I had to seize it. I rang the doorbell quickly before I could change my mind. I heard footsteps approaching and got ready to face Emily's mom, but to my surprise, a girl about my age answered.

"Hey, can I help you?" she asked, looking at me. I looked at her. She was close to my age and shorter. She had brown hair that fell to her shoulders and big brown eyes. It was like looking at my twin. This had to be one of Emily's sisters-my sisters, I thought. Where was the other one? I knew she had two.

"Is your mom here?" I asked. I was kind of hoping she would say she was at work or something so I could just come back later, but the girl turned and yelled for her, telling her someone was at the door. Then she walked away without a word, leaving the door open a crack. Suddenly it opened. A tall woman with dark brown wavy hair stood there. She was wearing black yoga pants and a blue zip up hoodie. She looked like she was heading to a gym.

"Can I help you?" she asked.

I looked at her, knowing I had to say something.

"I...I came here because you told the police...." She cut me off and narrowed her eyes.

"It's you. The girl who went to the police and told them you're our missing Emily," she said, keeping her voice low. It wasn't a friendly voice, and she definitely didn't sound happy to see me. "It took me a minute to recognize you because you pulled your hair back. Why would you even come here? I have two daughters who have grown up without a sister for nearly their entire lives, and you have the nerve to come here and pretend you're her? Is this some kind of sick joke?"

"It's not a joke," I said. "Look, I can show you some things." I dug through my backpack and pulled out the newspaper articles, pushing them towards her. She closed the door and stepped onto the porch.

"These are newspaper articles. They prove nothing. Anyone could have these." She turned to go back in the house, opening the door. She stepped inside and went to close it. I stuck my foot in the door to stop her.

"But could anyone have this?" I asked, pulling back my hair to reveal the small, jagged scar above my right eyebrow. I leaned close to her and stared at her with big brown eyes that looked just like hers.

"No…it can't be," she said, looking at me again. "We saw the photos the police sent." She opened the door a bit, and I removed my foot. "You…look nothing like her," she said, stepping outside and glancing back at the door. "I don't want my daughters to hear us talking. They're probably upstairs, but still."

"Look, I know this hair is really different. I dyed it, but when I saw this newspaper article and the picture, it was like looking into a mirror. I felt like I was seeing a picture of myself."

"But this makes no sense. If you are really her, someone would have found you long ago. According to the police, they either locate most missing kids within a few days or not at all. Our Emily has been gone for almost 10 years. There is no way you can be her. I don't know who you really are, and how you even got our address, but you need to leave now before my daughters come downstairs." She turned to open the door and go inside. This was my last chance. I opened my mouth and everything came spilling out. I could hardly get the words out fast enough.

"Look, I know it's crazy, but you have to believe me. My name is Emma. At least, that's what my mom told me. We live in another state, and we move a lot, like every few months. I don't have a birth certificate and no other family. Not a dad or any aunts, uncles or cousins, which is pretty weird, and she refuses to let me go to school. I can't even go to the movies with my friend, or the mall or anywhere. I'm not allowed to go anywhere without her. I'm pretty sure she's been lying to me all this time. Sorry, but no one believes me, not you or the police. I'm in a city where I know nobody. Someone mugged me and took all of my money. My mom called the police back home because I ran away a few days ago, and my best friend is covering for me, but I think her mom is getting suspicious, and…"

"Stop," she said, holding up her hand. "That's a lot to take in. It just can't be true. The police said…but we keep looking and hoping. That's why we went on TV."

"I saw it," I said. "I saw the interview on TV after the police kicked me out. Then I got some help from this woman I met and I told her everything I told you, and she said I had to be brave. She helped me find your address, so here I am. Please, please talk to me."

"We can't talk here. I don't want my daughters to hear us," she said. "Let me grab my purse and I'll tell my daughters I'm going to the gym. I'm dressed for it. There's a coffee shop at the corner. Meet me there. Then you can tell me everything, but this had better not be a prank."

"It's not," I promised. "I just want to talk to you."

A few minutes later, I sat alone at a small table in the corner of the coffee shop, glancing over at Marie, who was sitting in a nearby chair. She gave me a thumbs up just as Emily's mom walked into the coffee shop, spotted me, and sat down.

"Okay, talk," she said. And I did. Over the next 20 minutes, I told her everything I knew. I started with how I was looking for my birth certificate so I could go to school, and how I found the first newspaper article and about being confused why my mom had it since we didn't know anyone in Chicago that I knew of. I told her how I began questioning everything about my life. Then I told her about my Internet sleuthing, the plans Megan and I made, running away to Chicago, meeting Marie, seeing the police, and having them kick me out.

"So there I was with no money in a city where I knew no one. I was hungry and cold. All I had was Marie's number, so I called her. That's her over there," I pointed to the chair where Marie sat, hoping she would come over and help me, but she sat there engrossed in her book, or pretending to be. I'm sure she was hanging on every word. "She helped me find your address and said I had to come and see you because, obviously, the police are useless."

"What did you expect the police would do?"

"See that I look like Emily and give me a DNA test," I said honestly. "It happens on those TV shows all the time. They'd do the DNA, solve their case, and everyone lives happily ever after, except for the kidnapper, who gets arrested and goes to jail."

She shook her head. "The detective sent us a photo. My husband and I looked at it. He even printed it out, and we laid it next to pictures of Emily from when she was three. There is some resemblance, but we just don't think it's possible. Ten years is a long time, and missing kids just don't suddenly turn up."

"But they do sometimes," I said. "I remember there was a TV movie about this boy who was missing for something like seven years and he ran away and went to the police. They found out it was him and his family got him back. That could be me. I feel like I could be Emily. There are just too many weird things about my life that don't add up. My mom has no birth certificate for me, but she has hers, and there are no pictures of me anywhere. She said it all burned in a fire when I was three, but how would her birth certificate still be there?"

"Maybe she got a new one for herself for work, but didn't get yours?"

"Maybe, but what about how I have never met my dad, have no relatives anywhere, yet when I go missing, my friend tells me she made a phony phone call to my 'aunt' in Arizona. An aunt I had never heard of until that moment. She also didn't want to call the police when I went missing. What kind of mom does that?"

Emily's mom looked at me again. With a gaze locked on mine, she produced a photo of a little girl. Holding it up to her face, she lifted the hair so she could look at my scar. She touched it. "How did your mom say you got this?" she asked, tracing it with her finger.

"I hit my head on the corner of a coffee table when I was little. I must have been really little because I don't remember doing it."

"It looks exactly the same. I remember Emily was chasing her sister in the backyard. She slipped and fell, hitting her forehead on some rocks. I was gardening nearby, and she ran over crying. There was so much blood. I rushed her to urgent care, and the doctor had to give her stitches. The doctor had removed her stitches a month before someone took her. I had been applying cream to it, but it still left a scar. "

"It was the scar that made me think I was her," I whispered. "That and there was a bunch of stuff about my life that didn't add up when I really thought about it."

"Where do you live?" I told her I was from Colorado, but had always lived out west.

"So far away, and you said you move a lot?"

"Every few months. My mom. Her name is Diana. We move whenever she gets the urge. Sometimes she just comes home from work, starts packing and says we need to move right away. We only stay in places for a few months at a time. Six tops."

Emily's mom was quiet. "I can see how you might think something strange is going on. You seem pretty certain you are Emily."

"I am. If I'm not Emily, I don't think I'm Emma. I think my mom isn't my mom. I just need to prove it, and I need to do it quickly. My friend Megan and I were texting, and she told me her mom is suspicious and I think she's going to tell her where I am if her mom presses hard enough or calls the police and has them talk to her again."

"Speaking of the police, you said you asked for a DNA test?"

'Yep, and they refused. They think I'm a liar."

"I'm not so sure you're not lying, Emma, but everything you are telling me is so unbelievable. I just don't know what to do."

"Call the police," I begged. "Tell them I came to see you and you want to know if I'm lying. Ask them to DNA test me to see if I'm really Emily. Please!"

CHAPTER 20

After closing the door Emma's mom had left open after her abrupt exit, Megan's mom sat down on the couch and looked at her harshly now that they were alone.

"You obviously upset Emma's mom very much, Megan. Why on earth would you lie to both of us and to the police about being in touch with Emma all this time, and you helped her run away to Chicago? What on earth were you thinking? "

"I told you. It was an emergency. Emma had to do this, and I'm her only friend. I had to help her. So I gave her some money and helped her find out what train to take. She's fine. We have been in touch constantly."

"Exactly how have you been in touch? You told us that Emma didn't take her phone, yet the two of you have been texting, so obviously that was a lie too, one of many you have been telling."

Without a word, I stood up, went to my room, where I pulled Emma's dead phone from its hiding place, and returned to sit across from my mom. I plugged it into a nearby charger and waited for it to power up.

"This is Emma's phone. I had it turned off and hidden in my room where no one would find it. It's dead now, but I turned off the bluetooth and wi-fi and disabled the tracking her mom had set up, so no one would see it was here." I waited some more and soon the phone had a bit of power. "See? No messages between us recently." I held out the phone to her. She grabbed it with the long cord trailing behind it.

"So exactly how are you two texting, then?"

"Burner phone," I said, as if it was an obvious answer. "We bought it with some of the money I took from the bank. The rest went to pay for the bus ticket to get her to the train station downtown, the train to Chicago, and some money for her to get food while there. We figured she needed a few days to find out what she needed."

"Megan! What on earth were you two thinking? Of all the stupid things you have done, this takes the cake! Do you even know the worry you have put her poor mother through? You saw how upset she was when the police said they found all of your texts. You saw how she went pale and rushed out of here without a word. We need to go see her, and you need to apologize to her for what you have been putting her through."

"No!" I blurted. "We can't go over there."

"Megan, Emma's mom is very distraught and worried about her daughter's safety. We need to go over there and reassure her you will do everything you can to cooperate with the police to bring Emma home as soon as possible."

"I can't do that."

"Can't or won't? I cannot believe you and Emma did this. You said Emma needed to go to Chicago, and it was an emergency. You had better tell me what this is about right this second, young lady! Maybe I should call the police, have them come here and get it out of you!"

I paled, thinking of the two detectives grilling me some more. I had already faced that earlier, and I wasn't ready for another round. I knew what I needed to do, and I prayed Emma would forgive me. She was already on her way to see Emily's parents, I reasoned, so telling my mom-who would no doubt tell the police-will not change the outcome.

"Okay, I'll tell you, but you have to promise you won't tell Emma's mom," I pleaded. Remembering how her mom went pale when I mentioned Chicago, I added, "I'm guessing she might know exactly why Emma is in Chicago, anyway."

"What are you talking about, Megan?" my mom demanded.

I took a deep breath. "Emma is in Chicago because she's trying to find her actual parents." I let that sink in for a minute.

"She's adopted?" my mom asked, confused. "Did her mom not tell her, and somehow she found out? I still don't understand her running away to Chicago and why you helped her. Talking with her mom might have been a smarter choice."

"Not when her mom might have done something illegal," I said without thinking.

"What do you mean, illegal? Maybe I need to call the police," she said, reaching for her phone.

"No mom! No police, not yet. Let me just tell you everything first. I need to pull something up on your phone first, since the police have mine."

She handed it over. "I'm not promising no police, Megan."

I nodded. Then I did a quick internet search and found the original newspaper story about Emily, the one that Emma had found in her mom's files. I showed it to my mom and explained how Emma had found this very article hidden in her mom's files. She looked puzzled, so I quickly did another search and pulled up the more recent article.

"She wondered why her mom would have hidden the first article when they don't know anyone in Chicago and have never been there, so she did some searching online and found this article. It's almost the 10-year anniversary, so the newspaper ran another story and the police did an age progression photo of what the missing girl might look like today."

"I don't understand what any of this has to do with Emma," she said.

I sighed, unable to understand why she did not see what Emma and I had. "Look at the photo," I said, holding the phone up to her face. "Really look at it." As my mom did, I waited, but she shook her head. She was confused.

I rolled my eyes. "The girl looks just like Emma, same dark hair, dark eyes, and the same scar above her right eyebrow." Before my mom could argue, I went on about how Emma had met no family members ever, how she and her mom moved constantly, and how funny her mom was about her going anywhere in public, including school. "And she has no birth certificate for her, yet she has her own," I added smugly.

"Wait, a minute. She has an aunt in Arizona. Diana called and spoke with her."

"From another room, Mom. Seriously, don't you get it was a phony phone call? I told Emma about it, and she said she has no aunt that she knows of. Her mom was a foster child, and she never knew her dad. I'm telling you, mom, Emma's mom was faking it to throw you off and stop you from calling the police, but you called them anyway."

"So you're saying Emma ran away to Chicago because you both think her mother kidnapped her?"

"Yes."

"What I don't understand is why the two of you did not come to me with this information."

"Really mom? Was I supposed to just show you the news articles and say 'hey mom, we think Emma's mom kidnapped her 10 years ago'? Sorry, but you would have called the police within minutes, and they would call the police in Chicago, maybe questioning Emma's mom. No, Emma needed to go there and see what she could find out on her own."

"That's so incredibly dangerous, Megan. Something could have happened to her."

"Nothing bad happened to her," I said, pushing the images of Emma being mugged and alone in the city in the middle of the night out of my mind. "She met this woman on the train, a grandmother type who is helping her since the police there wouldn't."

"Where is Emma now?" she asked, picking up her purse. "You can tell me while I drive us to the police station, so you can tell those detectives all of this." She walked out of the door and I followed her. Was she out of her mind? The police would be more furious at me than before? Could they charge me with some kind of crime? Would they arrest me?

Those thoughts kept going through my mind as my mom drove to the police station, parked, walked inside, and asked for the detectives, telling the receptionist it was urgent. "It seems my daughter here has some vital information they need to hear." She and I took a seat, but it was just a few minutes before Detective Smith appeared. She gestured us to follow her to a small office where Detective Lewis was waiting and pointed to a pair of chairs. He did not look happy to see us.

"Talk," he said, looking at me, "and you had better not leave anything out." I told them everything. It all came spilling out so fast the detectives could barely take notes fast enough.

"Am I in trouble?" I asked in a quiet voice. I was shaking with fear now. Not only had I lied to them, but I had lied big time.

Ignoring my question, Detective Lewis asked where Emma was now.

"She went to see Emily's parents." My mom gasped. "Well, you can't blame her. The police there didn't believe her, so she did some digging and found the address where they live and went there."

Detective Smith looked at me. "I'm calling the police there. Maybe they can head her off before she does something stupid." She went to her computer, pulled up some information, and walked out of the room, presumably to make the call without us hearing her. Detective Lewis turned to me. "I'm assuming this is Emma caught on the train security cameras that day?" he said, pulling up a file on his computer. "There were a few teenage girls that time of day, but only one was Emma's age." I looked at the footage and saw Emma, shoulder length hair shoved under a hat with a backpack slung over her shoulder. She was standing against the wall as the train pulled up. She quickly got on the train, and it pulled away a few minutes later.

"That's her," I said to Detective Lewis as Detective Smith walked back into the room. He shook his head. "That matches the description of a girl the police in Chicago told me about. They had a teenage girl come in a few days ago, a runaway, but she didn't look like Emma. This girl had silver hair with purple streaks and refused to give her name, but she tried to tell them she was Emily."

My mom looked at me. "Silver hair?" she said? "I'm guessing you two colored her hair too?"

"We couldn't risk the cops picking her up. No offense," I said, looking at them. "I thought you would get a description out there and the cops would haul her back here," I said, looking at them.

"After the police listened to her, they took her picture and showed it to Emily's parents." I nodded as I knew about this. "Since you know we read your texts, you also know they kicked her out, thinking she was lying. We let them know she is in route to Emily's house, and officers are on their way there."

"It's too late," I said, looking at my watch. "She was heading there this morning to see Emily's parents. She is probably already there."

All three adults looked at me in disbelief. Finally, Detective Smith spoke. "This would have been good information to share with us the first time we talked to you, when you claimed to know nothing. Do you know how much time you have wasted? Not to mention the trauma Emma will cause Emily's family?"

"Emma thought they would believe her if they got to see her face to face," I said. "Maybe it wasn't the best idea?"

"You think?" Detective Lewis roared, his angry voice echoing through the small room. "I cannot believe you two kids did this! Do you know what kind of trouble you are causing?"

"We didn't mean to cause trouble. I swear. Emma just needs to know if she is Emily."

The phone rang. Detective Smith picked it up, listened to someone, whispered into the phone, and then hung up.

"That was the police in Chicago. They watched The Millers' house, and saw no activity, and didn't want to alarm the parents, but then Mrs. Miller called them. Emma confronted her and apparently was trying to convince her she is Emily. She is meeting Emma at a coffee shop, and the police are en route to take her into custody."

CHAPTER 21

Emma sat nervously as Mrs. Miller contacted her husband first to tell him what was happening, then the police. Mr. Miller was at his office in the city, and promised to come meet her right away, but insisted she call the police and not let Emma leave, not that Emma was planning to go anywhere.

From out of the corner of her eye, she saw Marie stand up and slowly approach them.

"Emma, is everything okay? I was sitting there watching you and you suddenly looked very nervous."

"And you are?" Mrs. Miller asked, looking at Marie.

"Marie. I'm a friend of Emma's. We met on the train when she came here, and I helped her find your address. I came here, and have been watching from a distance in case Emma needed my help."

"The police are on their way," said Mrs. Miller. "I gave my husband a call, and he said, 'Let's get the police on this. They'll know what to do.' Emma is insisting on a DNA test, but I'm not sure the police are on board with that. My husband and I do think it may be best, though.

Like me, he wondered if this might be a prank, but now I'm not so sure."

"It's not!" Both adults looked at me as I spoke up, unable to stay silent a minute longer. "Look, I don't know for sure I'm Emily, but there are too many weird things about my life that just don't add up. Maybe I'm not Emily, but maybe I'm not Emma either. I just know I need answers."

Before anyone could say anything, a tall, dark-haired man walked into the coffee shop, spotted Mrs. Miller, and embraced her before looking at me and then Marie.

"This is the girl? The one who claims to be Emily?" he asked. "I don't see it, but people can change a lot in 10 years." He studied me closely, and without warning, he moved the hair covering my eyebrows aside and looked closely at the scar above the right one. "Hmm...it's definitely a very similar scar, and it looks like it has been there for several years. How did you get it?"

I told him the story my mom had told me, not knowing if it was true considering all the lies she had told me throughout my life. I watched him for a minute, wondering what was going through his mind. Did he still have doubts like his wife, or were they believing I might be their long missing daughter? Would they insist the police give me a DNA test? I had tried that and failed, but maybe, just maybe, they could convince them.

Suddenly, I saw two police officers enter the coffee shop and approach us. "So...we meet again," one said. I realized it was the detective I had met with that first night in the city, the one who accused me of being a prankster and had thrown me out onto the street without caring what happened to me. He had accused me of being a runaway and had told me to go back home. I wanted to yell at him and tell him how he should have listened to me to begin with and given me a DNA test. I wouldn't have had to wander around the city at night, scared, hungry, and cold, afraid something was going to happen to me. I figured I had better not, as he did not look at all happy to see me again.

"Yes," I said. I wanted to see where this would go.

"You just couldn't leave this alone, could you?" he asked. "I don't know how you found out where the Millers live, but to go to their house took some nerve. They had already seen your picture and said they didn't believe you could be Emily, but you had to push it."

"I...I just thought if they saw me in person and not in a photo that they might believe me, that they might see that I look like Emily, and convince you to give me a DNA test."

"I already told you that wasn't happening," the detective said sternly. He ran his fingers through his hair. He had been on this case since the early days and wanted to solve it so badly. When Emily had first disappeared, he had young nieces not much older than her and the case had really gotten to him. He had pursued every lead that had come in, even the ones that seemed like they wouldn't plan out. When the young runaway had come to see him, his first impulse was to tell the receptionist to send her away, but he had talked with her and listened to her story. When he told her to go back home to wherever she had run away from, he never imagined she would stay in the city and somehow get to Emily's family. She was a lot more persistent than he had thought, and for a minute he wondered if maybe this was a lead he should have pursued, but it was crazy to think a missing girl would just appear a decade later. He realized the girl, both of Emily's parents, and an older woman were all staring at him. He needed to say something, anything. But what?

"Look," he said, addressing the girl. "What's your name? Your real name? I know you're probably a runaway and I'm guessing someone somewhere is looking for you."

Emma hesitated. She knew giving him her real name was not a good idea, because there was a nationwide alert for her out there as far as she knew, and she didn't match the description, but giving him her name might lead to him sending her back to Denver. She bit her lip nervously. "Fine," she said. "I'll tell you, but you have to promise not to send me back, at least not yet, please?"

"Why on earth would I do that?" he asked. Before he could continue, the older woman looked at him.

"Listen to me then, please," she said.

"And who are you and why should I listen to you?" he demanded. He did not know who this old woman holding a bag of yarn was, but she didn't seem like some stranger who was eavesdropping on their conversation, but neither of the Millers seemed concerned that she was there. He gestured to a nearby table and had them all sit down. The other detective stood nearby, making sure no one else entered the coffee shop. There was just one customer in the shop, who had earbuds in his ears and was working on his laptop, oblivious to what was happening. Two baristas were behind the counter, but not listening either, apparently warned by his partner to stay back. One walked over, locked the door and turned the sign to close.

Once everyone sat down, he turned his attention towards the older woman. "Who are you, and what's your involvement in this situation?" He pulled out a notepad.

"My name is Marie Davenport. I live in Slone Park and I met Emma on the train several days ago."

"Emma? So that's your name. What's your last name?" He asked, pen poised and ready to write.

"McKay," I said, reluctantly, knowing all he had to do was make a call or look up something on his phone. Then I would be in trouble. "Look, I will tell you everything, but you can't send me back!" I took a moment to decide how much to spill. "I'm from Colorado and yeah, I ran away from there. I met Marie on the train, but I gave her a different name, a fake one, you know? I didn't want her to find out who I really was in case she saw a news story about a missing girl. I thought I'd never see her again, but I did. It was after you kicked me out of the police station and accused me of pulling a prank. Which I'm not."

Detective Lewis gave her a cold state. "That remains to be seen."He stepped away and conferred with his partner in a whisper. The other man nodded and stepped to the back of the store, where I could hear him having a very quiet phone conversation with someone. I strained to hear what he was saying. He returned a few minutes later and looked at the detective.

"Emma Nicole McKay, age 13, reported missing from Falls Creek, Colorado, by her mother Diana. Here's the story," he said, turning the phone towards him.

Detective Stone turned to me. "Well, Emma McKay, now that I know you're not only a runaway, but an underage one at that, I'm calling the Falls Creek police and sending you back to your mom."

"No!" I yelled. "You can't do that. She may not be my mom. I think she stole me. I already told you about it when I first came to see you. I showed you these newspaper clippings and told you how I had found one hidden in my mom's files, and you laughed at me, told me I was playing a prank. You did nothing, so I took matters into my own hands. It's not like you were doing anything."

"Look, I know you think that's true, but I have worked this case for years," Detective Stone said. "I have spent hours interviewing witness-es and chasing down every lead. None of them panned out. Now out of the blue you show up and claim to be a missing girl from 10 years ago."

"You told me I was crazy and accused me of playing a prank!" Emma retorted. "I presented evidence and described my life in Colorado, emphasizing the lies I've been told. You blamed me for playing games and kicked me out! I found the Millers' address and went there to uncover the truth, since no one else would assist me."

Detective Stone sat there, stunned. This teenage girl, whoever she was, had a lot of nerve yelling at him like that. He really should send her straight back to Colorado. Still, there was something that stopped him. Maybe it was the way she glared at him with those angry brown eyes, or maybe it was that not once had she changed her story. Anyway, it seemed like the Millers, the only people he should think about, should have a say in the matter."

Before he could say anything, Mr. Miller said quietly, "At first when my wife called and asked me to meet her here and told me what was happening, that she had been confronted by a teenage girl claiming to be Emily, I wanted to dismiss it as a prank, but now that I have heard her story and see her in person, I'm wondering if maybe she is on to something. You have pursued many leads over the years, so what's one more?"

Mrs. Miller looked at her husband, and then Emma and Marie before adding,"I thought it was a prank too, and I was angry this girl just showed up at our door, but she was so insistent that I listened to her. I know it's a long shot, but I agree with my husband."

Emma held her breath and waited as Detective Stone took in what the Millers were saying. Would he finally agree to a DNA test? She had done everything in her power to convince him, and it hadn't worked, but now The Millers were her side, so maybe, just maybe, it would happen. Finally, he spoke. "Okay, Emma, you win. We'll do a

DNA test and find out if you're Emily Ann Miller or maybe someone else. Once we have answers, we can talk about what happens next." Detective Stone couldn't believe he was agreeing to this, but really there was no choice. The Millers wanted the DNA test, so they'd get one. He texted Michelle, the department's forensic scientist to drop anything she was working on and be ready to work on an urgent matter immediately.

CHAPTER 22

"Custody?!" Megan cried. "Why are the police taking her into custody?" Was Emma going to be arrested for running away? I was her accomplice. I had helped her plan this and gave her money, plus I had lied to the police. Was I in serious trouble too? We hadn't meant to cause trouble for anyone. Emma was my friend, and I had wanted to help her. Now we both might be in real trouble.

"Relax, Megan," Detective Smith said calmly. She was definitely the nicer of the two detectives, Megan thought, probably because she was a mom herself. She just had that calming personality, unlike Detective Lewis, who scared her. "Taking her into custody just means the police will go to the coffee shop where she is meeting Mrs. Miller and take her to the police station. We will work out transporting her back to Colorado."

"Without even seeing if she's the missing girl? Unbelievable!" Megan was angry. Not only were the police in Chicago involved, but Emma was going to be sent back to Colorado without ever finding out the truth. "It's not fair! She did all of this, and they're not even going to see if she is really Emily?" Megan stood up and walked across the small room and looked out the window, her arms crossed against her body.

"I'm not sure what exactly will happen, but seeing that Emma is a minor, I'm just saying we need to let her mom know she has been located and then..."

"NO!" Megan said a bit loudly. She turned away from the window and faced the two detectives. "Are you crazy? I told you Emma thinks her mom isn't her mom, but is a lady who stole her from her real mom, and you just want to send her back?"

"Megan, we don't know if any of this is true," Detective Smith said kindly. "There is no proof that Emma is a missing child. Just because she looks like some girl from Chicago who was kidnapped 10 years ago means nothing."

"I have told you it's way more than her looking like this girl," Megan said. "Before you call her mom, can you at least check in with the police in Chicago and see what's happening?"

"Megan, Emma's mom is probably worried sick about her," her mom said. "The police must tell her Emma is safe."

"Worried sick?" Megan was skeptical after seeing how Ms. McKay had gone deathly pale when she learned Emma was in Chicago and had rushed out of the room without saying a word. If Ms. McKay was worried about something, Megan would bet it wasn't about Emma being in another city, but why she was there. "Look, all I'm saying is Emma's mom hasn't exactly seemed too worried since she learned Emma was missing. She didn't even want to call the police until my mom pushed her. I'm just a kid, but that seems pretty suspicious. Then there was the phony phone call she made to her sister that I don't think exists. What if Emma is right, and she was the girl who got kidnapped years ago?"

Detective Lewis said, "If we don't find kidnapped children right away, the chances of finding them months or years later are very slim."

"But it happens, right?" Megan persisted, and the detective nodded. "All I'm saying is, it such a big deal not to tell Emma's mom what is happening in Chicago just yet? Maybe Emma met Emily's parents and convinced them she might be their daughter. Can you please call the police there and find out what's going on, or can I at least text Emma?"

"Fine," Detective Lewis nodded to Detective Smith, who walked out of the room to make a call. "Look, I know you two girls probably had good intentions, but not telling any adults what you suspected and having Emma see Emily's family without stopping to consider the problems it might cause is so irresponsible."

"We didn't mean to cause any problems. When the police there wouldn't listen to her, this woman named Marie she met convinced her she had to take matters into her own hands, so she did."

"Without thinking about the problems she might cause," Detective Lewis said. "Those parents have been searching for their missing daughter for 10 years, and some strange girl appears on their doorstep and claims to be her. I cannot even imagine how upset those parents are."

"Just think how happy they will be IF Emma is really Emily and they finally get their daughter back. They will not care how it happened. They will just be so grateful to have their daughter back."

"This is not some made for TV movie. This is real life, and missing kids just don't reappear years later and everyone lives happily ever after," the detective said, shaking his head. He looked at the door, wondering what on earth was taking Detective Smith so long. All she had to do was make a quick phone call to check what was happening in Chicago, then they could arrange transport of the minor and close this case that had taken up too much of their time. They had other, more important cases to work on. He had good intentions of sending Megan and her mom home, and was about to do that when Detective Smith rushed into the room.

"Sorry that took so long," she apologized. "Everyone better sit down for this, as a lot has been happening in Chicago. Emma somehow convinced The Millers that she might be their missing daughter, so the police have taken Emma to the police station to have a DNA test done, and they have asked us to hold off on calling Emma's mom just in case the test comes back showing Emma is really Emily."

"YES!" Megan pumped her fist in the air. "This is amazing! It is exactly what Emma was hoping for. How soon will they know? Can I call Emma and see how she's holding up? She must be totally freaking out now!" She reached for her phone, but the detective put his hand on her arm.

"No, not a good idea, Megan," he said. "There is absolutely no reason for you to be texting Emma right now. The police said the DNA test results are being rushed through, so they are going to call us once they know anything. Honestly, right now, the best thing for you and your mom to do is head home. If you see Ms. McKay, act like everything is normal and don't tell her you were down here. Act like you were out shopping or at a movie or something. If Emma is right and Ms. McKay kidnapped her, we are going to need to move in without her being suspicious."

"We'll do that." Megan's mom stood up. "Let's go, Megan. We need to stop and get a few groceries, anyway. That way, if we run into Ms. McKay, we won't be lying when we say we were out shopping."

Megan stopped at the door and turned to Detective Lewis. There was so much she wanted to say before her mom hustled her out the door to go to the store, but there was only one question she wanted answered more than anything. "What happens if it's true?" she asked.

He sighed. "That's a bridge we'll cross when we get there," he said. "Go home and we'll contact you when we have an update, although it probably won't be for a few hours. Megan, keep yourself occupied and hold off on texting Emma for now."

Megan's mom held out her hand, and Megan handed over the phone reluctantly. Megan felt tempted to text Emma, but she understood she couldn't. Her mom probably knew the temptation would be too much, so she had taken her phone. Despite not knowing Emma for long, they became close in the past months and she deeply missed her friend. They walked out of the police station in silence and made their way to a grocery store nearby. After they parked, Megan opened the trunk, took out some reusable bags, and followed her mom into the store. She felt relieved that her mom didn't talk to her. She most likely understood that Megan had no desire to have a conversation. Countless thoughts filled her mind. How was Emma, really? Was she freaking out? How was she feeling? Excited? Scared? Nervous? Megan wished she was with her at that moment. She wasn't sure what she could do, but her presence might have helped Emma. She started thinking about the DNA test. What if it showed Emma was really Emily? Would she go right back to living with that family as if nothing had happened? What would happen to Diana? She tried to imagine how it would all go down.

"Earth to Megan. Did you hear anything I said?" Her mom's voice broke into her thoughts suddenly.

"No, sorry. I wasn't listening. I was just thinking about Emma and wondering if she is alright. What were you saying?"

"I said, let's just pick up one of these fresh pizzas you like for dinner and a bagged salad. Nice and easy. Is that okay with you?"

Megan shrugged. Eating was the last thing on her mind right now, so she didn't really care, but she did like pizza, and the fresh ones from the grocery store were very good. "Sure, sounds good," she said, giving her mom a tiny smile.

They soon finished their shopping, walked back to the car, and headed to their apartment. The hallway was quiet as they got off the elevator, and Megan breathed a sigh of relief when she glanced down the hall toward the McKay apartment and didn't see the door open. Once inside, her mom opted to only turn on one small lamp in the living room before walking into the kitchen and turning on the oven.

Megan turned on the TV and flipped through the channels aimlessly, then switched it off, and picked up a book she had been reading earlier that day, but that didn't hold her interest either. She had too much on her mind. It was going to be a long couple of hours.

"Why don't you clear off the coffee table, and we will find ourselves a nice chick flick to watch while we enjoy our dinner?" Her mom walked over with two plates in one hand and some silverware in the other. Megan quickly moved the few things on the coffee table to an end table, and then walked into the kitchen and grabbed the bag of salad from the fridge, tossed it with some dressing, and set it in the center of the coffee table. Her mom set down a piping hot veggie pizza.

"That looks so good!" Megan grabbed a piece and put it on her plate with a pile of salad. For a few minutes, mother and daughter were silent as they ate their dinner. Megan's mom grabbed the remote, turned on The Hallmark Channel and sat back.

"This one is just about to start. It's about an American girl who falls in love with a boy who is a prince. It sounds good." Megan nodded, but she really didn't care. It was just nice to hang out with her mom and pretend this was a normal evening at home, even though they both knew it wasn't. She tried to relax and enjoy the movie, but her mind kept wandering to Emma. She wondered what was happening in Chicago and just how soon the police would know something. Detective Lewis had said the police in Chicago were rushing the DNA tests, but it still would be several hours before they knew anything. Megan hoped those several hours would pass quickly. She thought about Emma and wondered how she was holding up as she waited for the DNA results.

CHAPTER 23

Emma sat in the small room and looked around after the detectives had left. The room was obviously for visitors as it had a small TV, a collection of magazines, a basket of snacks, and a small refrigerator with bottled water. She thought about that afternoon's events. After quickly saying goodbye to Marie and the coffee shop and promising to call her as soon as she knew anything, Emma got into the car with the detectives parked nearby and left the coffee shop. It surprised her it wasn't a police car, but a plain, dark blue SUV. They drove to the police station where the DNA test would be done. Emily's parents drove their own car and would meet them at the station. As Detective Stone drove, the other detective, Detective Collins, told her they had been in touch briefly with the police back in Colorado, and had pieced together what had happened since she had run away.

"Your friend Megan was actually a lot of help," he said. "It helped the police there figure out where you were, and they called us."

"She swore not to say anything!" Emma was a bit upset at Megan for telling the police anything, but she supposed she should be grateful that it hadn't happened right away, and that with Marie's help she had located The Millers' house and met Emily's mom and then her dad. If she had squealed earlier, none of that would have happened, and the police would have probably picked her up and sent her home days earlier.

"She really didn't have a choice," the detective said after they arrived at the police station's parking lot. "Her mom suspected she was hiding something and took her phone. She had deleted messages, but the police could easily retrieve them."

Emma frowned. It was possible to retrieve deleted text messages? She thought about the number of messages she and her friend had exchanged throughout her trip. There had been so many. Had the police read every single one of them? She guessed they had.

"Anyway, the police there confronted Megan and she told them everything, and apparently begged them not to tell your mom anything. Your mom knows you are in Chicago, but that's all she knows."

"She is NOT my MOM!" I yelled. "I told you I think she stole me years ago." Emma was angry now. "This better not all be a lie that you're saying you're doing a DNA test, but you're actually sending me back to her."

"Relax, Emma," Detective Stone turned to her before getting out of the car he had parked in a reserved parking space at the back of the police station. "No one is sending you back to Colorado, at least not yet. The Millers have asked that we see if you are their missing daughter, so that's what we're going to do. Now let's go."

Emma followed the detectives into the station's back entrance. They walked down one hallway and then another before they stopped at a doorway. Detective Stone used his key to open it and ushered her inside. It was a small room with just a table and a few chairs. Detective Collins left, and soon returned with a short, dark-haired woman who introduced herself as Michelle Schultz, a forensic scientist. She had explained how the Rapid DNA test would work. It involved swabbing the inside of her cheek with a long cotton swab. They would then test it and match it with samples being taken from The Millers who were in another room.

"It's extremely accurate," she said. She explained that the testing wouldn't be painful and that the police would have results back in less than two hours.

"Then what happens?" Emma asked. That had been on her mind ever since the police had agreed to do a DNA test. "You didn't tell the police in Colorado, did you? They might tell my mom"

"The police in Colorado know, but because of the sensitive nature of the case, they are not telling your mom anything. They don't want to risk her taking off."

"Taking off? Like running away?" Emma felt shocked. "She wouldn't do that, would she?"

"Who knows?" Detective Stone said. "If she thinks the police are on to her, she might leave everything behind and go on the run. Now let's get this testing done."

The testing itself had been quick, but waiting around wasn't. Detective Stone had left with the forensic scientist, telling Detective Collins he would return once he had some news. They took me to another room down the hall, where Detective Collins sat, acting as my babysitter. He appeared unenthusiastic about receiving the task and promptly claimed the TV to watch a baseball game. I flipped through a magazine on the table, and then another. It had only been about half an hour since the test, so we wouldn't have results for a while still. I was so bored just sitting there with nothing to do, then I remembered I had a book in my backpack that I hadn't finished on the train. I opened my backpack, pulled out the book, and sat down in a chair near the TV.

Detective Collins sat in the other, completely engrossed in the baseball game he was watching on TV.

"Where are The Millers?" I asked him, my book down after a few minutes. I hadn't seen them when we had arrived at the police station, but I knew they had gone to another room, presumably to have a DNA test done.

"No idea," he said. With his eyes fixed on the game, he clearly had no interest in talking with me. "I'm guessing they did their test and then went home to wait for the results."

That made sense to Emma. It's unfair that they get to go home while she's stuck in this room, forced to endure a dull baseball game on TV. She glanced at her watch. Almost 45 minutes down and probably at least that to go. I was getting impatient. I reminded myself that I had waited this long, so surely another hour wouldn't kill me.

"Can I use my computer?" I asked Detective Collins hopefully. I figured that would be a no, but he didn't take his eyes off his baseball game.

"Look, kid, I just need to keep you in this room until I'm told otherwise. Do what you want to do. Just let me watch this game. It's the top of the 6th and The Cubbies are making a comeback."

With his strong desire to watch the game, it seemed like I could do pretty much anything as long as I stayed in this room and didn't bother him. I pulled out my laptop. Great, it was nearly out of battery. Spotting a nearby outlet, I plugged it in and waited for it to power up. Once it did, I did an Internet search for Emily Ann Miller + missing child. Nothing new came up. No news stories giving updates about the case. Then I searched for my name. Only the minor story about me missing came up and there was a grainy photo of me. I recognized it as part of one Megan and I had taken. How weird that there had been no updates to the story when I knew the police here had been in touch with the police back home. With Megan being questioned by the police and our texts being read, I had to find out what was going on. I was curious about whether they had given her the phone back. I thought it was fine to send a brief text. To be safe, I would keep it generic in case the police still had it.

Hey

Hey, What's up?

You got your phone back. I heard the cops took it and found our texts

Yep, apparently you can find deleted messages. Who knew?

Are you in a ton of trouble?

My mom's pretty mad at me for lying to her and to the cops. Cops said I'm not supposed to text, but my mom left my phone on the table. Make it quick.

So I'm with the cops now. Did one of those DNA tests. The parents asked for it.

And?

No news yet. They said 1-2 hours and we'll know. Parents did one too, but they're not here. They went home to wait.

What R U doing?

Hanging out in a room here with a cranky cop babysitting me. He's watching baseball. He told me he doesn't care what I do.

Nice. Crap! My mom's out of the bathroom. Gotta go.

Emma set down her phone and looked at her watch. She really missed Megan and wished they could have texted a bit more. She hoped Megan had deleted the messages so her mom wouldn't see them if she looked at the phone. What was the big deal, anyway? Why wasn't Megan supposed to text? Had her mom grounded her for everything? She hoped not. It was as much her fault as it was Megan's. They had planned this together, and it had all gone according to plan. Emma thought about her mom, well, the woman she had thought of her mom for her entire life. How was she doing? Was she worried about Emma? Was she bugging the police constantly for updates? Maybe she was, so it would look like she was concerned. If she was right and her mom wasn't her mom, would she take off before the police in Colorado could confront her? What would happen to her? Kidnapping was a crime, and this had happened 10 years ago? Could her mom still get arrested? Would she go to jail? Would there be a trial? Emma felt conflicted. She loved her mom. She was all she had in her life, and she was a good person. Emma didn't want her to go to jail. If she had stolen her, maybe there was a good reason. She wondered if the police would care. Maybe The Millers would be so happy to get their daughter back they would tell the police not to arrest Diana, but could they do that? Emma pondered this. Maybe if too much time had passed, the police wouldn't care, and Diana could go on with her life as if nothing happened. She assumed The Millers would take her home. How weird would it be to have to go live with some strange people she had never met in a state where she had never lived? How would that even work? Would they allow her to see Megan again, or would she have to say goodbye to the only friend she had ever had?

She was just thinking about how unfair that would be when there was a knock at the door, and Detective Stone walked in with the forensic scientist. Detective Collins reluctantly turned off the TV and motioned for her to join everyone at a table. Emma tried to guess what the detective might say, but the detectives' faces gave nothing away. Finally, it was Detective Stone that spoke.

"I'm going to just say it, Emma. The DNA test results are in," and he paused, placing his hand on mine. His voice had a slightly softer and kinder tone. The test results confirm you are indeed Emily Ann Miller."

CHAPTER 24

Emma let the news sink in. She had been ready for it to go either way, but deep down, she knew she had been right. Too many things about her life hadn't added up-things she hadn't really thought about by themselves, but when you put them all together and added in the hidden newspaper article and her eerie resemblance to the missing girl, it all made sense. Without meaning to, she sobbed. Detective Collins pushed a box of tissues across the table, and she took one, wiping her eyes as the tears continued. Finally, she spoke quietly.

"I...I can't believe it. Are you sure? I mean, could the test be wrong?"

It was the forensic scientist who had done the testing who answered. "No, it's not wrong. These tests are 99.5 percent accurate. There is very little margin for error, especially since we tested both of Emily's parents. Your DNA is a perfect match. Now we don't have DNA from your mom-well, the woman in Colorado that you have believed to be your mom all of these years, but I'm guessing if we did, the DNA would show she's not related to you."

"But, then who is she? Some random woman who lived in Chicago who just grabbed me when I was at the park? Then she took me to wherever far away, and somehow managed to keep me hidden away from anyone for almost 10 years.? How could that even happen?."

Detective Stone spoke up next. "We ran a background check on Diana McKay, and it came up clean. She lived in Chicago until almost 10 years ago, then she moved out West. Of course, we don't have a detailed background on her, or where she has lived these years, because that's not our concern right now. Our concern is reuniting you with your proper family. We called them a little while ago to let them know. Of course, they are in shock, but they are also so happy to have their daughter back. They're actually going to come here in about an hour. They were eager to come immediately, but we requested them to hold off because we expected it would be a major shock for you. I think we're all in agreement here - we're shocked as well. After a long time, we have successfully solved one of our most troublesome cases."

Emma wondered what would happen now. So The Millers just show up at the police station and she would go home with them? What about her sisters? Would they come with her parents to get her? She also wondered about Diana McKay, and what would happen to her now. There were so many questions running through her mind. She didn't know which one to ask first.

"So The Millers-my parents-are coming here soon and I will just go home with them? Is that how it works? They just come here, pick me up, and we head home?"

"Not quite, Emma," Detective Collins spoke. "Since we've solved a significant case, there will be a press conference today, including the family and you, of course. We let the Police in Falls Creek know, and they notified The FBI."

The FBI? Why? My puzzled look didn't go unnoticed by the detectives, and it was Detective Stone who provided an answer to an unspoken question. "You were a victim of an interstate kidnapping, where the kidnapper transported you across state lines. The Federal Kidnapping Act classifies it as a federal crime. Despite it occurring nearly a decade ago, Diana McKay will face federal charges. The FBI is on their way to your apartment to arrest her. Afterwards, they will transport her back to Chicago, where she will face formal charges and remain in jail until her trial."

"Arrested? Jailed? A trial?" Emma asked. "What will happen to her?" Emma felt shocked to learn that Diana had indeed kidnapped her, but she didn't think Diana was a horrible person. She had actually been very good to Emma and had taken excellent care of her over the years. Did that even matter?

"Well, I'm not up on federal law, but the penalty for interstate kidnapping would be very severe, I'm sure. It's a very serious offense, so I'm sure the FBI will want the maximum penalty as will your parents. It's not something you need to worry about right now."

I was worried though. I wondered what had made Diana take me all those years ago. Had she planned to steal a child? Had she been at the playground for that purpose and perhaps watched young children, looking for one that would be easy to steal? Maybe it had been an impulsive decision on her part. I imagined I wouldn't know until the FBI talked with her. I wondered if I would ever see her again. Probably not, I thought. I wasn't sure I wanted to anyway. She wasn't my mom, but she was a stranger who had stolen me from my mom. Now I was feeling angry. I had lost out on having a true family for almost 10 years while Diana dragged me all over the western United States. I had been deprived of not only a mom and dad, but two sisters, and I'm sure I had grandparents, aunts, uncles, and cousins. I had been deprived of a normal childhood, and now at almost 14 years old, I was supposed to just return to this life I didn't even remember to live with complete strangers?

"So how long until there's a trial? Will I have to go to it?" I asked, even knowing that Detective Stone probably had no idea, and I was right.

"No idea, but I'm sure a trial will be months away. Who knows? Diana may just plead guilty, and they may sentence her in federal court. There may not even be a trial. If there is, the prosecutor will reach out to your family and tell them what they need. Honestly, don't worry about that right now. Just focus on getting ready to see your family again and getting to know them when you go home with them after the press conference. They should be here soon. We will let you reconnect first, and then we will go over what will happen with the press conference."

A phone rang and Detective Collins walked over to pick up the call. I heard him talking quietly for a bit, then he hung up the phone and turned to Detective Stone. "Two things. First, the FBI picked up Diana McKay at her work. The neighbors informed them about the diner where she worked, as she was not at home. With no trouble, she was located and apprehended. The local FBI office will accompany her back to Chicago and assume control. They will transport her to a jail in the local vicinity and keep her there until her court date for the kidnapping charges. Two, The Millers are waiting in the conference room, just the parents. They left their other daughters at home."

Detective Stone turned to me. "It's time, Emily," he said, using my real name for the first time. "Your parents are really eager to see you and talk to you. We'll give you an hour in our conference room. That will give us time to let the newspapers and TV stations know there will be a press conference today to give them an important update on an unsolved case." He stood up and walked through the door. I picked up my backpack, slung it over my shoulder, and followed him out the door and down a hallway.

Suddenly, I was feeling nervous. I glanced down at my outfit, and wished I was wearing something nicer, but I had only brought casual stuff with me. My clothes were clean, thanks to Marie washing them. Marie! I hadn't told her the news. I needed to tell her. It wasn't right for her to hear it on the news for the first time. After all she had done to help me, she deserved to hear the news from me. So did Megan, I thought. Reaching into the pocket of my jeans, I felt for my phone and pulled it out quickly. I decided a group text would be best in this case, as I had little time. Detective Stone stopped abruptly at a door and turned to me.

"Wait," I said. "I just need a moment." Without thinking about how to say it, I typed a quick text message to Marie and Megan.

> DNA back. I'm Emily. Press conference on news soon.

I shoved the phone in my pocket and nodded to Detective Stone, who opened the door. Before I could say anything, Mrs. Miller crossed the room quickly with tears in her eyes. She pulled me into a tight hug, refusing to let go, and stroked my hair.

"Emily, I can't believe we have you back after all of this time," she said. "You have grown into such a beautiful young woman. I'm not sure I love the hair though. It's quite unusual."

"It's definitely different," I said, feeling awkward about how to address this woman I barely knew. Was I supposed to call her mom? "Maybe we can have it changed back?"

"We can talk about it," she said as Mr. Miller came over and hugged me as his wife let go reluctantly.

"I have to say, this is all such a tremendous shock," he said. "I still can't believe it. When we got the news, we called your grandparents. Both sets of them are still alive. Your one grandmother is letting all of your aunts and uncles know. Of course, we told your sisters too. They're so excited to meet you later today."

"Do I need to meet everybody all at once?" I said, beginning to panic. Going from one person in my family to a bunch was quite overwhelming and not at all something I was ready for. "Can I maybe just start with my two sisters and meet everyone later?"

"Of course," Mrs. Miller said. "We know this is going to be so hard for you, and our family needs to get to know you again first. We'll likely invite everyone over next weekend after we've settled you in at home. I figured you'd want to wear something nicer than jeans and a hoodie, especially with the press conference, until we have time to go shopping.

I grasped the bag, sat at the table, and pulled out the clothes. There were a few casual and really cute dresses, a pair of flared brown pants, and a few tops. I chose a short dress with a green and blue floral pattern and held it up to myself. It looked like it would fit. "I like this," I said. "The thing is, I only have these shoes." I pointed to my dark gray Converse shoes.

"It's fine, Emily. Your sisters wear Converse with dresses all the time. Why don't you go into the bathroom across the hall and change, and then we will visit a bit before the press conference."

I took the dress and my backpack and walked into the small bathroom.

***

Mrs. Miller watched her walk out of the room and looked at her husband and smiled at him. She was so glad she had decided to talk with this girl-her Emily-and then called her husband to meet her at the coffee shop. She was grateful they had pushed the police for the DNA test too, because without it, they wouldn't have their youngest daughter back. Once again, they were a family of five.

Inside the bathroom, Emily quickly pulled on the dress. She looked at herself in the wall mirror. It was a perfect fit. She wondered which sister it belonged to. She decided to leave her hair in its French braid as it looked nice. She applied a bit of lip gloss and mascara, looked in the mirror, satisfied, and returned to the room to join her parents.

"Hi," she said, smiling shyly, feeling like they were still strangers.

They both smiled at me. Time passed quickly as we chatted before the press conference. They were actually cheerful people, and I looked forward to getting to know them and my sisters better. We didn't talk about the kidnapping or much about my life in the past 10 years. They asked about my friends, and what I liked to do for fun. I told them I only had one friend, Megan, who I had known for just a short time, but we were close. I told them I hoped Megan and I could stay in touch. They said I could, and that made me happy. I knew I would make more friends, but Megan was important to me, and I would have been so upset to lose her friendship.

Before long, Detective Collins walked back into the room. "It's time," he said. As we walked to a side entrance to the police station, I saw a small platform had been set up. It held a few chairs and a podium with a microphone. As we got closer, I realized that the area was quickly filling with people holding cameras. I realized they were most likely from different newspapers and television stations. Suddenly, I felt very nervous and quite scared.

Mrs. Miller squeezed my hand. "Just stay close to us," she said. "You don't need to say anything unless you want to." She gave me a smile, and I tried to smile back. Then we headed outside. As we walked, I saw flashes of light and realized my picture was being taken by everyone.

Chapter 25

Megan and her mom sat glued to the television. The local news station did not have a reporter at the press conference, of course, but she recognized where the reporter was standing. It was just outside their apartment building.

"Good evening, I am standing outside of an apartment building where earlier today the police arrested and charged Diana McKay, a local woman, with the kidnapping of a little girl named Emily Ann Miller." Emily was just three years old when someone took her ten years ago from a park in Chicago. They named her Emma, and she has been living in this apartment building for the past few months, after moving here from Denver, where they had lived for a short time. We haven't found out where they lived before, but it seems their time in the state hasn't been too long." I held my breath and waited to see if I was going to be mentioned, but I wasn't. Too bad. It would be cool for me to be interviewed by a TV reporter. I said as much to my mom, but she quickly shot the idea down.

"Absolutely not Megan. I know eventually a reporter might dig around and find out you and Emma are friends, but if they ask to talk with you, it will be with me sitting right next to you and deciding which questions you will answer. I'm sure someone may eventually figure out Emma and you were friends. One of our neighbors who has seen you together in the hallway will talk."

I figured as much. My mom was pretty protective of me. Still, I thought it would be cool to sit down with a reporter. I could tell all of my friends to watch the show. They had never met Emma as her mom had never allowed her to go to the movies, hang out at the park or at the coffee shop. We could only hang out in one of our apartments, and our meeting had been a fluke as well since Emma had rarely left the apartment.

I looked at the TV. Now, the reporter was saying something about going live to a press conference in Chicago. After DNA results confirmed Emma was actually Emily, they held the conference and reunited her with her parents, who had been searching for her for almost 10 years.

"Wow! There are a lot of reporters there," I said as the screen switched over to the press conference. I could see Emma sitting next to a couple. The woman was holding her hand. Emma was wearing a pretty dress I had never seen before, with her hair pulled back into a neat French braid. She looked incredibly nervous and a bit scared.

We watched as a tall, gray-haired man in a shirt and tie stepped up to the microphone. "Good afternoon," he said. "I am Detective Stone with The Chicago Police Department. Thank you all for coming on such short notice. I had said we have an important update about an unsolved case...That case is the disappearance of three-year-old Emily Ann Miller 10 years ago. She had disappeared while at Bessie Coleman Park with her mother and sisters, and we have had many leads over the years, but none panned out until now. I'm happy to report that the case is closed, and Emily is now back with her parents. At this time, I will give you a bit of information about how this case was solved, then I will take some questions. From what we have learned from talking with Emily, Ms. McKay moved around frequently, never staying in the same town or often the same state for more than a few months. She lived under her own identity, and had worked in several restaurants, most recently in a suburb of Denver. "

He went on to explain that Emily had discovered some information that led her to believe that she might really be a missing girl, and had run away to Chicago and come to the police station to tell them who she thought she was. He didn't add anything about the police not believing her, or her finding her parents' address on her own and confronting them. I supposed he didn't want to make himself look bad. He simply said that rapid DNA testing had been done on Emily that confirmed her identity.

"Now, I will take some questions," he said, introducing Detective Collins as someone who had assisted on the case.

A reporter from The Chicago Tribune raised her hand and was called on by the detective.

"Where is Ms. McKay now? I assume someone has taken Ms. McKay into custody?" she asked. I could see her holding a small tape recorder up as she spoke.

"That is correct. Once we had an identification of Emily from the rapid DNA test, she let us know the address where she had been living for the past several months. We got in touch with the local police, who we had already been in contact with. They contacted the local FBI office, which arrested Ms. McKay without incident. Authorities charged her with interstate kidnapping, and they will bring her back to Chicago to face those charges."

He took a second question. This time from The Chicago Sun Times. Enthusiastically, a young man asked, "Did you say that Emily had discovered some information that made her believe she was a missing child who had been kidnapped almost a decade before?"

Detective Stone paused. "No school has ever registered Emily as a student. Ms. McKay insisted on homeschooling her, she told us. When she began wanting to attend school like other kids her age, she looked for her birth certificate in some files while her mom was at work and came across a newspaper article from years ago about this missing girl. Like any teenager, she is good at using the Internet (The reporters laughed.). She quickly found an updated article a newspaper ran recently where one of our police artists had created an age progression photo. Emily saw it, and noticed she bore a very close resemblance to the missing girl, right down to a small scar above her right eyebrow. She did not want to confront the woman she believed to be her mom, so she and a friend hatched a plan to have her run away to Chicago, which she did a few days ago. This all happened quickly."

He looked at the reporters. "Right now, I am going to have Emily's parents come up and make a brief statement. They will NOT be answering questions today."

Mrs. Miller, who was still clasping Emily's hand, looked at her husband, who stood up with her and Emily. He took Emily's other hand and nodded to his wife, and they approached the podium. He let go of Emily's hand and spoke.

"My wife and I, on behalf of our daughters and our entire family, wish to thank The Chicago Police Department for all they have done to solve this case. We never for one minute gave up hope our Emily was out there someplace. Now that we have her back, we ask for privacy as our family gets to know each other again. After all, we knew Emily as a little girl in preschool. She is now a teenager who will celebrate her

14th birthday in a few months. We want to get to know her, and for her to know us. For that, we ask for privacy. Thank you."

He turned to Emily, took her hand once again, and said, "Let's go home."

CHAPTER 26

The car ride back to The Millers' house was quiet. I was grateful that The Millers didn't try to talk to me. They still felt like complete strangers to me. So much had happened in such a short amount of time, and so much about my life was changing so fast. Less than a few weeks ago, I had been living in Colorado with a woman I believed to be my mom. Then I discovered that newspaper article hidden away that had started me on this journey. Megan and I had planned my running away so carefully, and I had gotten away with everything so easily and had been able to find out the truth that I had suspected from the start. I held onto my cell phone tightly, the burner phone Megan and I had bought to stay in touch. My real phone, the one connected to Diana McKay's account, was hidden away in Megan's room and really wasn't mine anymore. No doubt it would be disconnected soon anyways. It didn't matter. There wasn't anything I needed on it. I imagined I would get a new one soon. At least I hoped so. I wonder if The Millers believed in 13 year olds having cell phones.

We pulled into the driveway, and slowly got out of the car. I looked at the house, the pretty flowers in pots by the door, and the swing. It looked like the perfect place to read. I couldn't believe that I would actually get to live here in an actual house. After a lifetime of living in different apartments every few months, I was going to live in a house! I was going to live with a family! Before we reached the front steps, two teenage girls came running out the front door. I recognized the one as the girl who had opened the door for me earlier that day. A slightly taller girl, with short brown hair who looked a bit older followed behind. My sisters!

"You're home!," the younger one exclaimed. She pulled me into a hug, and I stepped back shocked that this strange girl was hugging me. "Sorry, I'm just so excited to see you again! Do you remember us?" I looked at the girl who was close to my age and looked so much like me. I wished I did remember her or anyone in the family, but I didn't.

I shook my head and replied, "sorry, it has been a long time. I was just a little kid."

"It's okay. I'm Jessica. I'm 14, almost 15." I was confused, as I had thought she was younger than when I had seen her that morning at the door. She was a few inches shorter than me. "I know, I'm so short! Everyone always thinks I'm younger than I am, but I'm almost exactly a year older than you. Our birthdays are a few days apart."

"That's pretty cool." I looked at the older one. She was a lot quieter than Jessica. Her short, brown hair was parted to one side, and long bangs hung to the side. She wore oversized glasses on her tiny face. She gave me a smile.

"I'm Samantha," she said, "you can call me Sam for short. Sorry if Jessica freaked you out. She can be too much" She rolled her eyes. "I'm going into my last year of high school and I'm 17."

"Wow," I said. 'You look so much older, and you're so tall." She was several inches taller than me.

"I'm 5'9, and no, I don't play basketball or volleyball before you ask. I'm an artist."

"Wow, that's really cool! I love to draw!"

Mr. Miller, who had been listening to our conversation, suggested we all head inside the house. I followed everyone inside, and stood there, not sure what to do. Luckily, the over enthusiastic Jessica was right there. "We should give Emily a tour of the house," she said. "Maybe she will remember something."

"Lead the way, Jessica," Mrs. Miller said. "We'll follow you girls."

I followed Jessica up the stairs, and I noticed the wall was lined with family photos in frames. I saw a few pictures of the three of us girls, frozen in time at ages 7, 4, and 3. I stopped and stared at it. Then I saw a photo of all five of us with the girls in the same outfits. We all wore matching floral dresses, and the same shoes.

Holding back tears, her mom mentioned, "That photo was taken a few weeks before...before you vanished." "Your dad had just hung those two pictures up a few days earlier. It's the last picture we have of you three girls together."

"We should have another one taken!" Jessica said. "But not in matching dresses." I laughed at this, knowing she and I agreed not to wear matching clothes.

We walked upstairs with Jessica acting as tour guide. She quickly pointed out the bedrooms where she and Samantha slept, our parents' bedroom, and then the one I had slept once slept in. I stepped inside. It was as if time stood still. This wasn't the bedroom of a teenage girl, but that of a three-year-old. I despised the pink color that someone had painted the room with. White sheer curtains tied back with pink ribbons hung on the big window that overlooked the backyard. The bed was so tiny! I would never fit in that! I'd probably break it if I sat down on it. A small white wood table with chairs sat in the corner, a stuffed bunny sitting in one chair. A dollhouse sat in one corner. I picked up the bunny and held it to me, smelling it.

"That was your favorite," Samantha said. "You dragged it everywhere. You actually had it with you that day at the park, but you dropped it. The police found it when they started looking for you. We brought it home and put it right there. It has been there ever since."

I looked at the very worn, gray bunny. It had a bit of pink on its ears. "I'm guessing I really loved this as a kid? It looks pretty old."

"You got it as a present for your 2nd birthday and slept with it every night," her mom said. "You're probably too old for a stuffed animal now."

"I am, but I like this one," I said, reluctantly setting it back right where it had been for 10 years. "This room is like a museum. You didn't change it to a guest room or something?"

"No. I wanted to keep everything exactly as it was. We thought the police would find you right away, but they didn't. I used to come in here a lot those first several months. I would sit on your bed, hold your toys, and wonder where you were. After a while, it got too hard to be in here, so I would come in less often. I know it's a baby room. We'll change it however you want. We can paint the walls, change the curtains, and get new, bigger furniture."

I looked at the room one more time. I had never lived in a place where we could paint the walls, and the only decorations I had ever had were drawings I had tacked up on the walls. It would be nice to have a cute bedroom where I could hang out, something like Megan had back in Colorado, I thought.

We went downstairs and saw the kitchen, laundry room, and an enormous room they called a family room. There was a set of stairs. I peeked down there.

"That's the rec room," Mr. Miller said. "We have some comfy chairs and a big TV. The girls like to hang out with their friends down there." Wow, a whole room just for hanging out and watching TV or playing games. That was pretty cool.

We all sat down in the family room. It was a large room with a few cozy couches and some chairs. A large TV sat at one end, and a fireplace at the other end. Mrs. Miller had gestured to the couch when we had walked in, so I had sat there. Jessica sat on one end, and Mrs. Miller on the other. Mr. Miller and Samantha sat in nearby chairs. Mrs. Miller opened an enormous book she had pulled from a bookshelf. "This is an old family photo album. I thought maybe you would like to see more pictures."

"I would," I said, pulling the album closer and flipping carefully through the pages. She had labeled everything. I saw pictures of myself as a baby, sitting on a different couch with my sisters. I saw pictures of me surrounded by a bunch of kids. I looked at Jessica, puzzled.

"Our cousins," she said. "That's Michael, Joey, Andrea, Elizabeth, and Shannon." They all live pretty close. "Michael and Elizabeth are brother and sister. They belong to Uncle Jim and Aunt Wendy. Joey, well, he goes by Joe now since he's 17 and thinks he's too cool. Andrea, and Shannon belong to Uncle Mike and Aunt Susan."

Cousins. I had cousins. I had aunts and uncles. "Do they live near here?" I asked.

"They do! Can we have everyone over for a party, mom?" Jessica asked eagerly. "I can make a cake!"

"Let's hold off on that, Jess," she said. "Your poor sister is probably already feeling overwhelmed. We'll reintroduce her to the family gradually."

"Thank you," I said. "I'm sorry. This is a lot to take in. Since I can remember, I've only had one person I thought was my mom. It used to be just the two of us, but now I'm returning to a family and a house that is unfamiliar to me. I have cousins, aunts, uncles, and grandparents. It's a big change, and I'm kind of freaking out. Would it be okay if I just went upstairs to chill for a bit in my room?"

"Of course," Mrs. Miller said, squeezing my hand. "Girls, let your sister just be by herself for a bit. We'll order some pizzas for dinner in a few hours. Emily, do you want a snack?" I shook my head and stood up.

"Oh Emily," Mr. Miller said. "I know that bedroom furniture is really tiny. We have some air mattresses the cousins use if they spend the night. Just for tonight, I'll set one up in your room, then tomorrow we'll get you some furniture and talk about what you want to change in your room. Jess, get her some bedding, please."

I had been in here for just a few minutes when Jessica knocked on the door and waited for me to give her the okay to enter.

"I won't stay long," she said, setting down the bedding on the air mattress. "I know you just have that backpack with a bit of clothes, so I brought you a pile of some of my clothes since we're the same size. You can wear whatever you want until mom takes you shopping. Oh, and you can keep that dress," she added, pointing to the one I had worn for the press conference. It looks way better on you than me." She closed the door and left me alone.

I changed into a pair of black yoga pants and a green T-shirt. I placed the other clothes and the dress on top of the dresser, put my shoes on the floor next to it, and lay back on the mattress and stared at the ceiling. So much had happened in such a short time. I was glad no one was forcing me to keep hanging out downstairs. I needed some time alone.

Before going to bed, I sent a quick text to Megan, hoping she had her phone back and would respond.

Hey

Hey! Saw you on the news

This has been a crazy day

Yeah

I can't believe my mom is not my mom

I know

Its so weird being here. The one sister Jessica is super friendly. I think she expects we'll be besties. I don't even remember her.

And the other one?

Samantha. She's quiet and an artist like me. She hasn't said much

You alone?

Yeah, I told them I needed space. I'm in my old room. It's pink

Eww

They said I can change it, but…

But, what?

It's so weird being in the room I slept in when I was 3. It's a total baby room and I am living with complete strangers. Did I make a mistake?

No, Definitely not. It's your family

But, Diana is, I mean was my family. Now she's in jail. I feel bad, like I put her there.

She did this, not you.

I just hope I can fit in.

You will. Stay in touch.

K

I stared up at the ceiling, so many feelings were hitting me all at once. I felt happy to be home, but also a little sad for the life I was leaving behind by returning to this one. I also was nervous and scared about what lay ahead. I sat up and walked over to the little table and chairs. I picked up the stuffed bunny and hugged it to my chest. I looked at the dollhouse and the tiny furniture it held. I opened the closet where dresses hung on little hangers. These were a little girl's things, and I wasn't a little girl anymore. Being gone for 10 years from this life, I had missed so much. I was a completely different person now, and I wondered how I would fit back into my new life.

Acknowledgements

This book would not exist if not for the encouragement of a few people who have mentored or encouraged me along the way.

Thank you to fellow writers Marie Secoy and Elisabeth Chretien who have been great mentors, and helped me take a half written story to a finished one. Thank you to my long time friend and romance writer, Victoria Hamel for showing me that self-publishing was possible, and for answering lots of questions throughout my journey to become a published author.

Thank you also to my beta readers Stasia Coleman and Onyinyechi for reading an early copy of the book and giving me valuable feedback that helped shape the final version of this novel. Also, a huge thank you to Lori Miller for editing the book.

I also want to thank author Kasie West who I met at a book signing several years ago. When I told her about my book I had just started, she encouraged me to finish it, and signed her book for me, saying she couldn't wait to read mine some day. I'm hoping she reads this one!

Thank you to my readers for picking up this book, and giving a new author a chance. I appreciate you!

Please follow me on Instagram at author_colleen_bergquist for updates on my writing and opportunities to read advanced reader copies of my future books.

ABOUT THE AUTHOR

 Colleen's love of writing began in middle school where English was her favorite subject. She always wrote short stories in notebooks, and dreamed of writing a novel some day. An avid reader, she spent most of her childhood with her head in a book, often reading two and sometimes three books at a time-something she does still today.

A native of the Chicago area, Colleen has called the suburbs of Denver, Colorado home for nearly a decade. She and her husband have two sons and two dogs.

She has a masters in Elementary Education, and teaches full time. When she is not writing, she loves to read, crochet, and watch reruns of *The Gilmore Girls*.

Reunited is the second book in *The Stolen Trilogy*.

Find her on Instagram at author_colleen_bergquist. Follow to get updates on her writing and have a chance to be an advance reader for future books.

If you've enjoyed this book, please take a few minutes to leave a review on Amazon. This will take you to a page with all of the books in the trilogy.

https://mybook.to/StolenTrilogy

ALSO BY COLLEEN BERGQUIST

The Stolen Trilogy
Stolen (Book 1)
Reunited (Book 2)
Confrontation (Book 3)

www.ingramcontent.com/pod-product-compliance
Lightning Source LLC
Chambersburg PA
CBHW061528310726
48972CB00008B/2372